SUSPENSE AT ITS BEST . . .

HOME AGAIN
David Wiltse

"YOU'LL BE ENJOYING
THE ABSOLUTE MASTER
OF THE PSYCHOLOGICAL SUSPENSE GENRE."
Larry King

"*HOME AGAIN* IS A SPLENDID READ;
INTELLIGENT, PERCEPTIVE
AND ALSO THRILLING."
Robert Daley, author of
Prince of the City and
Year of the Dragon

"A REMARKABLE MYSTERY"
Booklist

"WELL WRITTEN . . . SENSITIVE . . .
WITH A GOOD DEAL OF ACTION"
Newgate Callendar,
The New York Times

HOME AGAIN

David Wiltse

 AVON
PUBLISHERS OF BARD, CAMELOT, DISCUS AND FLARE BOOKS

This novel is a work of fiction. Names, characters, places and incidents are either the product of the author's imagination or are used fictitiously. Any resemblance to actual persons, living or dead, events or locales is entirely coincidental.

AVON BOOKS
A division of
The Hearst Corporation
105 Madison Avenue
New York, New York 10016

Copyright © 1986 by David Wiltse
Front cover photograph by Joel A. Meyerowitz/TIB
Published by arrangement with Macmillan Publishing Company
Library of Congress Catalog Card Number: 85-31845
ISBN: 0-380-70392-0

The Macmillan edition contains the following Library of Congress Cataloging in Publication Data:

Wiltse, David.
  Home again.
  I. Title.
PS3573.I478H66   1986   813'.54   85-31845

First Avon Printing: August 1987

To my wife, Diane,
with gratitude forever for
teaching me about love

Chapter 1

My father was hunting someone when I was born. He was always hunting someone in those days. It seemed to be a perpetual open season for him. My mother was attended during the final few weeks of the pregnancy by her *mother, the two of them mending their brittle relationship long enough to see me born before reverting to their postures of self-righteous victimization.*

My father didn't see me until I was eight weeks old. He returned to Helena in the middle of a frigid Montana winter, bearing no baby rabbit skin to wrap his baby bunting in, but just another notch on his record, another citation for meritorious hunting. He was with us while we moved to Des Moines—another in a long series of dreary temporary postings—staying only long enough to see the moving van off; then he, too, was off, leaving my mother to cope. She became very good at coping.

It went that way for the next fourteen years, posting to posting, hunt to hunt. There was something persistently rural about my father, some combination of taciturnity and bluff candor that made him uncomfortable in a large city, so the assignments were always to the lesser capitals, Helena or Casper or Bismarck. The Bureau was not interested in his comfort, of course, only in his effectiveness. He disapproved of so much in the cities—not only the men he sought, but all of the random corruption, the sleaziness, the tawdry, indifferent *depravity of city life—*

that his distaste made him visible. Visibility in a hunter is a serious flaw, so after a few abortive attempts to change him, the Bureau kept him consigned to the hinterlands, where he could move unseen and silent.

He never spoke of his work when he was home. He might have been a banker or a carpenter for all he ever said about himself, but I managed to follow his career in the local papers, decoding small headlines and brief, undetailed stories. "Agent does such and so." "Such and such a gang thwarted."

Just before my fifteenth birthday, he made front pages, nationwide.

The dogs had been sent for. The men had been waiting over an hour, a ring of hard-eyed agents surrounding a half-demolished, bullet-ridden house, tired and annoyed now that the shooting had stopped. The surge of adrenaline had passed, leaving them uncomfortable and nervous. They had pumped the house full of tear gas, and tendrils of it puffed lazily through the holes in the wall whenever a breeze blew. The gas had not worked, and each wisp of it served as an irritating reminder of the failure. The men were angry and growing increasingly frustrated, but the decision had been made to use the dogs and there was nothing to do now but wait for them to come.

Slapped down in haste by a poor but ambitious farmer who did most of the work in his spare time and only managed to complete the structure six weeks before being evicted, the house had been erected without a basement. The foundation was a set of concrete blocks at each corner of the house and several more blocks positioned under what the farmer guessed to be the major stress points. His guess had been as poor as his luck. The ground had begun to settle even before he was finished, and the house now sagged on its frame, the weight-bearing timbers bowing downward like wet cardboard.

Judging by the construction, there should have been nothing between the house and the earth but a crawl space to allow for inspection of the pipes. But, as the agents had discovered to their surprise, there was a cellar beneath the house, dug by the present occupants and reinforced on top by thick concrete to form an impenetrable bunker. The occupants were in their redoubt now, armed and murderous.

Special Agent Pete Ketter stretched out on the ground with his back to the wheel of a squad car that was between himself and the line of fire from the cellar. There was little danger. The terrorists would have to poke above the floor to shoot, and they hadn't done that for the better part of an hour. In the beginning, shortly after going underground, they had tried a few offensive moves, lifting just their weapons above the trapdoor and firing blindly, hoping to hit anyone not under cover, or at least to discourage any further movement toward the house, but they had soon given that up.

The agents had blasted huge holes in the walls, carving them out with close-to discharges of riot guns, creating a skein of openings that provided the agents with a clear view of the interior of the house, which now had the appearance of a colander with a roof. From one angle or another, every square inch of the interior could be covered with fire and the agents had long since riddled every stick of furniture, every closet, and every cabinet that could possibly hide a person. Even the refrigerator lay on its side, victim of a shotgun blast, its contents spilled on the floor like intestines. That frenzy of firepower had taken place after the tear gas failed, but it had been no more effective, apart from ventilation. The terrorists had already turned turtle and drawn into their shell.

Two attempts were made to approach the trapdoor, and both had resulted in agents being shot through the floorboards. One had been saved by his protective vest, and the other was rushed to the hospital with part of his foot gone. Since then, the battle had turned static, like the siege of a castle.

Ketter looked up languorously at Special Agent-in-Charge Meisner, Ketter's nominal superior, who paced agitatedly back and forth behind the squad car. Meisner *looked* thoughtful. Ketter believed that Meisner's great talent lay in looking thoughtful while not actually thinking at all.

"Can you hear anything?" Meisner asked.

Microphones had been laid atop the floorboards and every movement underground could be monitored. The agent wearing the headphones was named Holz.

"They're still singing," said Holz.

"The bastards," muttered a policeman. He looked at Meisner for a reprimand. The agents made an issue of courtesy and politeness, and all the state and local police surrounding the house were under Meisner's control in this operation.

"What are they singing?"

Holz lifted one headphone from his ear, as if he could hear better that way. "Something about taking his time," he said, "because that is the kind of guy he is."

Ketter chuckled. Meisner turned on him.

"Is there humor there, Ketter?" Meisner demanded.

"A little bit," said Ketter. He smiled lazily, irritating Meisner further. "They know you're listening."

"*We're* listening. We. Or am I in this by myself?"

"They're just trying to get to you," said Ketter.

"They're not getting to me," said Meisner angrily. He lifted his binoculars and scanned the house for the fiftieth time. "They're the ones who are trapped in a hole in the ground, surrounded by who-knows-how-many agents and police. They're the ones who are going to do federal time for about thirteen different offenses. Not me. They're not getting to *me*."

"Probably you're getting to them, which is why they're singing," said Ketter.

Holz looked away quickly, avoiding Ketter's eyes to keep from laughing.

"Probably got those people hunkered down in there in that hidey-hole, wondering, 'What on earth is Meisner going to throw at us next?' Which is why they're singing snatches of Hoagy Carmichael. It *is* just snatches, isn't it, Holz?"

Holz turned his back to Ketter and busied himself with the knobs and dials on the amplifier. His shoulders shook.

"I mean, they're not singing the whole song, for heaven's sake."

"They're trying to goad me," said Meisner. "They'd like me to waste them. But I'm not buying it. I'm not out to make any martyrs to their cause. We'll wait for the dogs."

"I think it's Gershwin," Holz volunteered, deadpan. He held his expression while Ketter wriggled his back against the tire, trying unsuccessfully to scratch an itch through his protective vest.

"You mean they've got Gershwin down there with them? These people will stop at nothing!"

Holz made a sound like a man being strangled.

"I mean Gershwin wrote the song," he managed to say. He quickly turned away from Ketter again, but the laughter was already burbling out.

"You had me worried," said Ketter. "Gershwin is dead."

"Agent Ketter, you're beginning to wear me out," said Meisner. He scanned the house through the binoculars once more, then sat between Ketter and Holz. As Special Agent-in-Charge of the district of the Dakotas, Meisner was, nominally at least, Holz and Ketter's superior. Meisner held no illusions about his abilities as a law officer, however. It was widely acknowledged that Ketter was the best in the district when it came to detective work or police action. Ketter was the one who had located their present quarry after six months of patient and exhaustive work and brought them to ground. Politically, however,

Ketter was a disaster, and Meisner shone. Ketter won citations, Meisner got promoted. Meisner was aware of the inequity and, on occasion, troubled by it, although never enough to relinquish command.

"We'll wait for the dogs," Meisner said again, as if to convince himself.

"Sound, very sound," said Ketter.

"All right, let's hear it."

"Hear what, Special Agent Meisner?"

"Get off my case and tell me what you would do if it were up to you."

"Can't think of an improvement. Absolutely outstanding performance thus far."

"If you want to tell me, Ketter, then tell me. Quit slopping the heavy-handed sarcasm all over and just come out with it."

"Well . . . one little thing. I might have tried to grab them before getting on the bullhorn and ordering them to come out with their hands up."

"I wasn't aware they had dug a goddamned bunker under the house."

"No, indeed."

"Well, did *you* know it?"

"I knew they've been loose for three years with half of the law officers in the country looking for them. I knew they'd been cornered in New Jersey and escaped. I knew they had access to Uzis, grenades, and very probably a rocket launcher, and I might have guessed that they'd have gas masks since they had them in New Jersey, and I knew these were some very desperate and unfriendly people who've already killed two armored truck guards and did their best to kill a couple of New Jersey state patrolmen, and I knew they've had several months at least to get this house ready, and I think I might have tried some approach other than circling the wagons around the house."

"They haven't gotten away, have they? This is no New Jersey deal here."

"We haven't got them yet, either," said Holz.

"Did I ask you, Holz?"

"I was just saying."

"We'll get them," said Meisner without conviction. He picked up a pebble and hurled it into the distance, then fell silent for a moment.

"So?" he said after a time.

"So what?"

"So, how would you get them out?"

"Me? I'd wait for the dogs."

"Goddamn it, Ketter, I'm *asking* you!"

Ketter stood, looking down at Meisner until the other man rose. Ketter was an inch over six feet tall, a good-looking man with dark hair and a nose that was just large enough to lend a sort of unorthodox distinction to his face. His was the kind of face other people not only liked, but remembered. Ketter kept his eyes on the house as he spoke so Meisner had to lean close to hear him.

"The dogs are a waste of time," said Ketter. "They're good for tracking or defense. We don't need to track, and we don't need defense. They're just dogs, not ferrets. We know where they are. They're in a hole they've dug for themselves. These people are asking you to come and get them and, like it or not, that's what's going to have to be done."

"We can starve them out," said Meisner.

"If they had sense enough to dig the hole, don't you think they had sense enough to stock it with food and water? They're probably ready for a siege."

"They can't last forever."

"They don't have to. Keep them trapped for a week and they get a week's worth of headlines. National headlines. Six-o'clock news. 'Yahoos still foil FBI.' 'Yahoos release demands.' 'Yahoos hold out for the seventh day.' It's the kind of publicity they'd die for. And I mean that. They're prepared to die for it. They're not just bank robbers, they're fanatics."

The wind gusted and a spiral of gas, like grayer air, corkscrewed out an upper window. The tear gas was heavy, designed to hug the ground and disperse slowly, but it had been released more than an hour ago and gradual mixture with the surrounding air had thinned it out. It looked to Ketter like heat shimmering from a road, visible only because it moved.

"So?"

"So, you're going to have to get them out," said Ketter. "Unless you want a national incident."

"I didn't know you cared about the politics of these things," Meisner said.

"I'm not a politician." The contempt was heavy in Ketter's voice. "I'm not a plumber, either, but I care about sanitation."

"It's a girl's voice now," said Holz.

"Marianne Fleming," said Ketter. He had seen her photograph so many times he could conjure a picture in his mind of the whole person: the texture of her hair, the quality of her skin. She had the strained smile of her Swarthmore graduation picture: a tense, serious girl trying to oblige the photographer with the mandatory grin. Ketter had envisioned many changes about her—different clothes, hairdo, makeup—the many, easy, everyday disguises a woman would use to make a plain face pretty, a pretty face plain, or simply different. He had, in his mind, played with her face like an artist, painting on lips, stretching eyebrows, pulling the hair back severely, letting it fall softly to the shoulders, highlighting the cheeks, lining the eyes, altering the appearance in many different ways so that he could recognize her in any crowd. But he had never been able to do much with the mouth. At times he thought he knew the face of Marianne Fleming so well that he could smell the shampoo in her hair and feel the sweet warmth of her young breath—but always with the same tense, uncomfortable smile. He never saw her laughing in his mind.

"What's she singing?"

" 'Big Rock Candy Mountain,' " said Holz.

"Burl Ives," said Ketter. He remembered the record in her last known apartment, the folk singer's goateed face gazing out from a blue background. The album cover was dog-eared, the record deeply grooved from use. What could it have meant to her? A legacy of her parents? A gift from her boyfriend? Fleeing from the FBI and the police, she had taken the time and trouble to carry an album of folk songs with her. Ketter did not know why, but he knew that in some curious way he admired her for it.

"The buzzing of the bees and the cigarette trees," Holz sang in accompaniment. "The soda waa-ter fountains . . ."

"Shut up," Meisner said irritably.

"She has a lovely voice," Holz said wistfully.

"Does she?" Ketter took in the information, filling in his picture still more fully. Marianne Fleming of Weston, Massachusetts—only child of Dr. Carl Fleming of Weston and Mrs. Erica Fleming Uedess of Boston and Miami Beach, graduate of Swarthmore with a major in English literature and a minor in computer science, model student, loving daughter, hospital volunteer, who emerged one day as arsonist, bomb builder, and getaway driver—had a lovely singing voice. One piece made as much sense as any other.

"You'd think they'd go for rock," Holz said. He was forty-one, the father of a teenage son, and he equated contemporary rock with sloth, insubordination, and heroin.

"They're complicated," Ketter offered.

"How do I get them out?" Meisner asked. He kept his eyes on the house and his tone casual, as if he weren't pleading for rescue.

Ketter turned and studied Meisner for a moment, but the special agent never looked away from the house. His profile was blunt, falling almost directly from forehead to chin without disruption by a nose, as if the maker had run out of material. From the side, Meisner looked like a bulldog, Ketter thought, but without the courage or the resolution. They had worked together for two years, and in that time Meisner had been promoted twice, while Ketter had been passed over twice.

Ketter dropped a hand on Meisner's shoulder. "Command decisions, Special Agent. Hazards of the job."

Meisner smiled bitterly. He hadn't expected Ketter to save him.

"The dogs are here," said the policeman as a pickup truck with the bed converted to a kennel bounced over the open ground toward the squad car. The dogs began to bark loudly with anticipation, their sounds drowning out the few scattered hands clapping in derisive applause. Meisner was the only one with any hopes for the dogs.

The dogs were Alsatians, bred for controllable ferocity. They leaped out of the truck like wolves after prey, but at a command from their handler they stopped and squatted, their ears down in submission. Trained to obey their handler without hesitation, as eager for approval as children, they were also trained to attack other men, to slay or die in the attempt. Seeing Eye dogs, narcotics sniffers, shepherds, pets, killers. A marvelously versatile animal, Ketter thought. It all depended on what they were taught, on how those traits of courage and tenacity and intelligence were shaped and twisted. Like heated metal extruded through a die, they became man's best friend or a beast that hunted men, depending upon the forces applied. What forces had twisted Marianne Fleming? he wondered. What pressures had been applied, and who had applied them, to take her dedication, her intellect, her compassion and convert them into this, a twenty-five-year-old, ash-blond lover of folk music, sitting in a hole in the ground with an Uzi on her lap, hunted by dogs? The equation would never balance for Ketter. Whatever had happened had done so quietly and internally and completely, and Ketter had never found a clue or a witness to the transformation.

* * *

It was a ludicrous attempt. The four dogs, lean, strong, and savage, were helpless under the circumstances. The crawl space was too low for them to stand erect, thus negating their strength and speed. The remnants of the tear gas mingled with the scent of the terrorists and confused them. The terrorists saw them coming, heard them coming, waited, then destroyed them.

The agents heard a burst of rapid fire from an Uzi, followed after a pause by another burst. They automatically took cover at the sound of shots, and a few bullets that missed their target whined out from the crawl space, ankle high. A stray shot hit the tire of the squad car, which blew out with a startled gasp.

One of the dogs whined for half a minute, then the agents heard a single shot and all was quiet. The single shot was from a pistol, low caliber, a .32 or .38, and Ketter wondered which of the terrorists had shown the compassion to dispatch the wounded animal. Was it Marianne? She had owned pets as a child. He had seen pictures of her in the family album, a girl of ten hugging an Irish setter. Then later, a teenager, wires on her teeth, looking up, startled by the camera, her lap filled with a wary-looking cat and a very young puppy. She had kept that snapshot in a frame on her desk. There were no photos of her parents. A picture of pets, a satin pillow in the shape of a heart, a stuffed animal once in the shape of a bear but long since squeezed out of any recognizable form, eyes gone, material rubbed thin—but no sign of a family. What forces? Ketter had interviewed both of the parents extensively. They seemed like decent, caring people. What war had gone on between them to drive them to divorce, and was Marianne a casualty of that war?

It took Meisner the better part of an hour to placate the dogs' handler. The stunned man listened to Meisner's soothing, politic tones at first with no comprehension then growing rage as the size of his loss sunk in. By the time he fully realized he had lost not only four dogs but his major capital resource, the man was screaming at Meisner, the FBI, the U.S. government.

Meisner dragged him away from the others, still speaking calmly in the hushed voice undertakers use for consoling bereaved relatives.

"This is terrific," said Holz. "We got five of the most wanted bastards in the country in a hole, surrounded by umpteen peace officers and four dead dogs and what is our valiant leader doing?" The handler's voice erupted furiously in the distance, demanding justice and revenge, to be taken not from the hide of the killers but from the backside of the government in general and Special Agent Meisner in particular. He would burst forth at intervals, exhaust himself with outrage, then subside as Meisner's unctuous tones poured more oil upon the waters. "He's struggling to apply a lip-lock on the love-joint of a highly pissed-off dog man."

"Never easy," said Ketter.

Holz laughed. "If Meisner would just drop his pants and spread his cheeks and let the guy ream him, it wouldn't take so long."

The police officer laughed uncertainly. He was not sure if he was allowed to be amused by the Bureau.

Holz continued to make fun of Meisner but Ketter ceased to listen. He was thinking of what was going to happen next. The sun was fading and the sky, which had been a brilliant blue, was draining of color. A few clouds, hanging low to the horizon, turned pink, like puffs of cotton candy. The birds began their frantic evening chorus, proclaiming their territorial rights one last time before dark. It was too beautiful a time for killing.

Meisner returned to the squad car at last and summoned the other agents. The police maintained the chain around the house while the Bureau conferred.

"We have a light problem," Meisner said. "It's going to be dark here pretty soon. We don't want to take any chances on their slipping out, so we're going to point all the squad cars directly at the house and use the headlights and searchlights to keep them pinned down.''

"They'll shoot out the lights,'' said Ketter.

"Then we'll use flares! This is not going to be New Jersey all over again! They're not getting out of here!''

"Get some more dogs,'' said a voice from the rear of the group. Others chuckled as Meisner glared.

"I'm open to suggestions,'' he said grimly. "Provided they're serious.''

The men stood silently. The siege had gone on too long already; they were beginning to feel foolish.

"Use the darkness,'' Ketter said resignedly. He knew the result before he stated the solution.

"I was thinking about that,'' Meisner said quickly. "That's a possibility. A very real possibility. They can't see us any better than we can see them. Someone could slip in under there and get at them.''

The men avoided each other's eyes. They were family men with wives and children, men who had been trained as lawyers and accountants before joining the Bureau. They had learned to deal with weapons, to face danger on those occasions when it could not be avoided, but there were no kamikaze pilots among them.

Meisner looked them over, savoring the power. He had their full respect for the moment, and they feared him.

"Ketter,'' he said, a trace of relish in his tone. "You know them better than anyone else.''

Ketter said nothing.

"You've been tracking them, you ran them to earth here. I imagine you feel a sense of responsibility about them.''

Ketter stared at Meisner, his eyes calm, expression blank.

"We all know you're a brave man, you've got the commendations to prove it, but I don't want you to think you have to do this just because of that. You mustn't feel compelled to demonstrate your courage again. That is not necessary.''

Meisner turned so all the men could hear him clearly. He was establishing his alibi. "This would have to be voluntary. If at any time you feel you're in unacceptable danger, you back right out of there."

Ketter continued to look at Meisner, now with a slight smile as if watching the amusing gyrations of a biological specimen before piercing it with a fixing pin. Meisner found the gaze and the silence unnerving.

"Of course, if you'd rather not, we'll all understand." Meisner looked at the others, polling them for approval of his understanding and compassion.

Ketter was actually paying little attention to Meisner. He had known it would come to this, every mistake Meisner had made had led inexorably to this conclusion. He was thinking instead of Marianne Fleming. All men who hunted for survival felt a kinship with their prey. Indians made totems of the buffalo, had visions of them, thought of them as brothers. They worshipped what they sought. Ketter felt some of that for Marianne.

He looked upward. The sun had gone completely and the sky was turning bluish-black. A crescent moon hung low over the horizon, shining bone-white, and Venus, the evening star, twinkled between the cusps, emblem on a nocturnal flag.

Meisner had drifted into silence as he realized Ketter wasn't listening, and now he waited, they all waited, for Ketter to decide.

Ketter looked at the house. Its shape was beginning to lose definition at the edges where wood met night. Underneath it, the blackness of the crawl space was darker than the surrounding area, like the mouth of a cave on the side of a black mountain. It was not the way he had hoped to meet Marianne Fleming.

The redoubt under the house was not an actual bunker as the agents believed, but several connected trenches that had concrete roofs only at the extremity of each trench.

The terrorists could stand under the roofed portions and be secure from fire from above, which had to pass through floorboards and several inches of concrete, or they could step into the open portion of the trench and shoot up through the floor or horizontally through the crawl space. They could not see to fire and be fully protected at the same time, but they could move quickly through the trenches to reinforce one another and sit out any attack in relative safety. They were fanned out under the house at the tips of a five-pointed star, armed with enough ammunition to slaughter an entire police force, provisioned with enough supplies to last nearly a month.

Although trapped with no reasonable expectation of escape, they were in good spirits. The final confrontation had come at last, and they felt a sense of exhilaration at being able to make an end of all the running, the hiding, the ceaseless paranoia. As any martyr knew, sacrifice is easy once one has accepted the inevitability of it. The five remaining members of a fanatical group of radicals that had never numbered more than a few dozen were now accepting their suicide with the kind of joy known only to the self-righteous.

Marianne Fleming felt a curious sense of peace. She knew that she should probably be frightened, but after the initial shock when Kareem had grabbed her from bed and shoved her into the tunnels, her emotions had been so mauled by the events that it felt now as if nothing could disturb them again. She had been terrified during the firefight when the FBI had all but blown the house apart, then panicked when she caught the first burning whiff of the gas. Her mask had been impossible to get out of the bag, her fingers clumsy and half-paralyzed with anxiety. She had been certain the mask would not work and she would succumb to the gas and then, seconds later, equally certain she could not withstand the claustrophobia that the mask clamped on to her like a hand across her face. But the mask had worked and she had withstood the claustrophobia. When she heard the floorboards overhead creak with the weight of the FBI men, she joined the others in firing a volley blindly upward into the wood.

The others were elated, particularly Kareem, who had longed more than any of them to draw blood at last, but Marianne was relieved. She had prepared for this action for months, but she was not ready for the reality. From the very beginning she had been worried that when the time came she would cower and tremble and turn from the revolutionary that she called herself into the frightened little girl that she suspected lurked forever in her heart. But now she had survived it, she had not run screaming into the arms of the pigs, she had not crumbled or begged. If she was not a hero, at least she was not a fraud. There was nothing left now but to hang on for a time and then, when the FBI made their final rush, to die.

Marianne hummed "Goober Peas" softly as she peered into the darkness of the crawl space, the song subconsciously bringing her the same sense of comfort and serenity as when it had played endlessly on the phonograph in her childhood room. Her parents had raged and fought in other rooms, their angry voices and tense hostility cutting through her door while she squeezed her eyes closed, pulled the pillow over her head, and hummed along with the record until she fell asleep, at last.

There was little to see even during the day, when only the tires of cars and occasionally a man's foot had passed within her line of sight, but at night the weight of the whole house seemed to press down upon her vision until she was seeing the whole world through a tiny crack. The bullhorn crackled an electronic noise for a second before the man's voice boomed out. It was the same voice that had been alternately urging and demanding that they surrender all day.

"This is your last warning," the voice added. A new development.

"I hope it is, man!" Marianne recognized Kareem's voice, high and cracking when he was excited.

"You're boring us to death!" Arthur Lumpkin. He was almost giggling with exhilaration. She could imagine his wild eyes, the way he looked around to others for confirmation. Except now there was no one to see him. She wondered if Arthur was high.

A shape seemed to materialize out of the darkness just before the edge of the crawl space and Marianne felt her stomach lurch. The shape moved again and positioned itself so that the concrete leg supporting the house was between itself and Marianne. She thought she saw a part of it sticking around the concrete, but it was so low to the ground, and now so still, that she wasn't sure. Was it a man? Were they coming after all? It still did not move and Marianne hoped she had been mistaken.

Cars were on the move now, she could hear them driving over the uneven surface of the yard, springs sighing. They moved with their lights off, but Marianne thought they were moving away from her side of the house.

Her friends were speaking softly to each other. She could hear Walter Stepgood, his slow Massachusetts accent sounding worried, as it always did. He had been the one who recruited her; slow, intelligent, concerned Walter Stepgood, scion of an old New England family. Her first lover, Walter had receded from her affections after she met Kareem and Arthur and Ned. He still visited her at night sometimes, making love with the same, hesitant, considerate style as the first time. It amazed her that she had progressed so much as a lover since her awkward debut with Walter, yet he had changed not at all. If anything, he was worse because her expectations were higher.

"Just hang tough. Watch your perimeters." The voice was Ned, their military commander, son of a career soldier whom he despised but struggled to emulate.

The headlights of five cars snapped on simultaneously directly behind Marianne. The others opened fire and Marianne whirled around and raised the Uzi. The other four points of the star were in front of her and she could not safely fire without endangering them. The headlights were shattered and darkness reclaimed them. When Marianne turned back to her own perimeter, her vision was worse because of the lingering effects of looking at the headlights. It took a moment to realize that the shape was no longer behind the concrete blocks. Anxiously she scanned the darkness, looking for any shape darker than the rest, any suggestion of movement.

There, to her left and five yards in front, was a hump in the black. She fired into the shape, the bursts from her gun illuminating the night for a few feet, but when they faded, she could see less than ever.

Kareem was beside her, touching her arm. She nearly shot him before she knew who it was.

"What the hell is it?" he demanded.

"I shot one of the dogs again," she said. "I . . . I thought I saw it move."

"Calm down, sweet thing." He put his hand on her cheek and she pressed against it, allowing herself the moment of comfort. Kareem's palm was moist and sticky.

"Just be cool, now. Be cool."

"I'm all right," she said, but she wished she could ask him to stay with her.

"I know that much," he said. "Don't worry about nothing, it's better to shoot too much than too little. We ain't trying to hide, they know where we are."

She nodded and he patted her cheek, letting his fingers trail slowly across her skin before he withdrew. Kareem was always tender with her except during sex. Then he was harsh and impersonal, the worst of her lovers.

They heard a hiss, then saw a bright light snaking toward them from the direction of the cars, traveling very fast and low to the ground. It struck the house just above the crawl space, fell to earth, and exploded into a blinding light. They're coming, Marianne thought, my God they're coming now, and she realized she wasn't prepared at all.

When the first flare faded, the agents shot another. This one landed under the house and ricocheted upward into the floorboards, where it struck, then burst into a hissing star of brightness. Marianne was blinded by the light. She closed her eyes and ducked into the trench, beneath her sheltering roof, but still the phosphorescent illumination seemed to sear through her eyelids.

The others were firing wildly, unable to see past the flare, and Marianne stood up to join them. As she turned to face her perimeter she could smell flames and she realized the house over her head was on fire. She lifted the Uzi and saw a man directly in front of her. The flare had bleached his features as white as a ghost.

"Marianne," he said.

She screamed as she fired, but he had blocked the gun with his arm so she was shooting aimlessly into the house. He wrested the Uzi from her hand and spoke her name again. The others were firing madly, yelling to each other, and Marianne wanted to call to them but her voice was already crying out in a prolonged scream she couldn't seem to stop.

She groped in her pocket for the pistol she had used to finish the dog.

"No!" the man yelled.

She pulled away from him and freed herself, inches from his grasping fingers. As she lifted the .32, the flare faded, rose for half a second in an afterglow, then vanished.

"No!" the man yelled again but Marianne did not stop. Then Marianne Fleming, who had plotted the destruction by force of the United States government while listening to Burl Ives sing about goober peas, was dead.

Ketter shot her in the face and then tumbled into the trench after her. The only light came from the flames flickering along the underside of the floorboards. Ketter felt for her jugular vein, hoping to find a pulse, but his hand came away slick with liquid. He paused for a moment over the body of the girl he had hunted for so many months, then lifted his head to fix the positions of the others. They were firing disorientedly now, panicked and completely out of their depth. For Ketter, taking them was the easy part.

Chapter 2

He would not talk about it. Two days after we saw the account in the newspaper, my father informed us that he had resigned from the Bureau. He had a degree in law, he announced, and it was high time he practiced it. Three days later we were on our way to Cascade, where he intended to join his brother's legal practice.

To me, it was just another move, as whimsical and arbitrary as all the others. Like a bird in a storm, I had no choice but to fly with the wind. I was fifteen, a sophomore in high school, an age when I already felt that most adult actions were wrongheaded and mean-spirited anyway. One more random jab of unfairness merely confirmed my view of things.

For my mother, however, this latest move provoked a sense of insecurity bordering on hysteria. She had spent her married life, she explained, devoting herself to the advancement of his career. She had played diplomat for him, boosted him to all who would listen, taught him— or tried to teach him—the social niceties that would smooth his path. (Her primary tool in the diplomatic department was a refined use of hypocrisy, an art she excelled in and my father, despite ardent coaching, never completely understood. His rectitude was an obstacle to politesse that she could never quite overcome.) She had done all this, plus put up with the abundant inconveniences of the Bureau life, and done it with flair and lack of complaint—according to her—but only because she wanted to help him advance himself. Implicit in the bargain, of course, was the assumption that he would continue to advance, not abandon it all and take up a new career at the age of forty.

Worst of all was the mystery of it. My mother did not love a mystery. Uncertainty of any kind made her nervous, but this action so agitated her that for several days she could not sleep.

"But why?" she demanded again and again. She would ask the question suddenly, abruptly, dropping it into a silence or the middle of another conversation, as if it had a priority that needed no preamble. "Why on earth?"

"It was time," he would say, nodding slowly as if delivering a large truth.

"In three more years you could have had a pension! Why couldn't you wait three more years!"

"It will be good for Mike," he said. "Cascade is the kind of place a boy can put down roots."

"I don't want any roots," I offered.

"Yes, you do."

"Cascade!" my mother said, her voice rising with frustration. She was from Columbus, Ohio, originally, a city that had come to seem enormous in size and sophistication after the series of lesser capitals where she had been forced to live over the years. "Cascade!"

"We can probably get you a job helping out on a local farm," he said to me, cheerily.

I stared at him, aghast.

"A farm?"

"Baling hay, driving a tractor. It'd be good for you, Mike." We were driving on Route 35 cutting a swath through the cornfields of Iowa. He reached over and patted my thigh. My mother had lapsed into silence in the backseat, preparing herself for another onslaught.

"I don't want to."

"Yes, you do," he said. He was very merry about it. He seemed to derive a particular pleasure from planning

a new future for me. The fact that I had no use for his plans didn't seem to faze him, or indeed even to penetrate his envelope of good cheer. In the few days since retiring, he had changed greatly. I had never known him well; he had been a laconic man, seldom home and only vaguely present when he was there. Now, however, fits of gaiety of a type we had never seen before would seize him, like a man who is all at once relieved of a heavy burden and feels he is suddenly walking on air; and he would become so happy, so antic in his good spirits that he would embarrass us. My mother was solemn to the point of gloom when she wasn't frantically assailing him for answers, I was uncertain and tentative about the latest change, but he was positively delighted with things. His cheerfulness greatly annoyed both of us.

My mother spoke up from the backseat, leaning forward so her mouth was next to his ear. "What happened?" she asked in a hushed tone, trying to create an intimacy as if I weren't there. "Please tell me what happened."

"High time for a change," he said. "A great place to learn responsibility, Mike-o, Mike-o, Mike-o." He tapped me on the shoulder, playfully but with a strength he was unaware of, then bounced his fist several times on the steering wheel. The prospect of hard work and responsibility—for me—seemed to please my father no end. As I had done increasingly over the past few days, I fell into deeply wary unrest. Even less than my mother did I understand what had caused the change in my father, but the thing that worried me the most was that it seemed directed toward me. He had taken all of the intensity and energy that had gone into being a hunter and turned them on me. I felt his attention like a heavy weight and was certain I would break under the strain.

We arrived in Cascade after a day and a half of driving. There were people waiting there, and signs, and some sort of delegation. It was the first time I realized that my father was a hero to other people, as well as to me.

They had gathered to greet the returning hero in a spirit of pride and friendship that had seemed to them, although they would never have said so, the very essence of small-town life. Under the direction of Bobby Hauck they had first cleaned the house and stocked the shelves with those simple necessities like matches and soap that housewives knew always seemed to get lost in transit. The moving van had arrived and with Bobby Hauck dancing attendance once again they had arranged the furniture so the family would arrive to a semblance of order. More than a dozen of them had helped in one way or another, and then they had waited for over an hour, their eager expectancy being slowly eroded by the heat of the sun.

Hauck was a short, plump man, with thinning hair and long, elegant hands. Although personally reticent, he relished social activity and delighted in gossip. From an early age, people had told him their stories, had seemed drawn to him by confessional urges, and Bobby had listened, his head cocked to one side, nodding with sympathy and understanding, while his slender fingers touched at their tips, forming a temple under his chin. It gave him the attitude of prayer and many of his confidants came away from a session with him feeling as if they had been truly understood for the first time in their lives. Women were particularly prone to confide in him and he had enough self-awareness to realize it was because he offered them no threat. He was as mild as any woman, as patient and sympathetic, and yet he was a man and thus, to many of them, possessed of the greater intelligence necessary to fully understand their problems. For most of the women who came to him, Bobby Hauck was their only chance to speak to a male sensibility without being judged. There was a tinge of illicit thrill that came with gossiping to Bobby—or rather gossiping at Bobby, for he seldom returned in kind—that made him not only a release, but an adventure.

For the men, he was just masculine enough so they did not feel uncomfortable with him, yet gentle and placid. They felt that they could unburden themselves of their tenderer emotions and weaker impulses without danger. If anyone would understand the softer sentiments, Bobby Hauck would.

In time, Bobby had turned his talent into a profession. He became a reporter and, eventually, the editor of the *Cascade Spectator*. People continued to talk to him. First they told him the facts, then their feelings. He published one, held the other.

When the Ketters finally arrived, Bobby was the first to greet them, smiling shyly at Pete Ketter as they shook hands, watching the other man's eyes shift from his face to the waiting crowd. Ketter was surprised, then flattered, and Bobby tactfully withdrew, allowing his old friend to deal with the situation in his own way. He watched from the back of the crowd as Ketter's older brother, Edward, shouldered his way forward, a beefy, florid-faced man with the instincts of a politician. Edward Ketter embraced his brother, then his brother's wife and son, holding each to him in the possessive hug of a loved one. Bobby knew Edward had seen none of them in ten years, nor cared to. Edward Ketter had a way of taking possession of an event merely by embracing it, and he did so now, placing an arm on the shoulder of his brother and his wife and walking with them toward the house—as if he had been responsible for the event, for preparing the house, for the gathering of friends, and not Bobby Hauck.

Now that their hero had arrived, no one knew exactly what to do. Bright expectancy had been dulled by reality. They stood clustered around the front porch, shuffling uncertainly on the lawn, their heels gouging little dents in the grass. Ketter and his wife stood on the porch, their son behind them, the boy's hand on the door of the house as if ready to flee. A banner of different colored strands of crepe paper hung from the lintel, hastily applied with tape that had failed, releasing a single red ribbon, which fell across the door like a spill of blood.

Janet Ketter broke the awkward moment as she had so many times in her married life—by taking charge. She slipped her hand under Ketter's arm, establishing herself as the wife of the hero, lady of the manor, and then beamed at them as if bestowing a baronial blessing.

"You must all come in," she said. She felt her husband's arm sag slightly. His idea of a proper greeting would have been to thank them all for coming, then go inside and close the door. But Janet had seldom let his ideas of social behavior prevail. She had a duty and she would perform it with style, head erect, smile fixed firmly in place—not too broad, no teeth showing, courteous and friendly, but reserved. She squeezed Ketter's bicep to give him strength, waited for him to open the door, then led the way into the house.

The people of Cascade responded to crises with food, and Pete Ketter's homecoming, a crisis of celebrity, had brought forth as much food as a death in the family. The women trooped into the house bearing platters and trays covered with aluminum foil, earthenware crocks sealed with heavy lids, and plastic bowls with transparent tops. They brought fried chicken and Jell-O molds, baked beans and brownies, enough to feed the Ketters for a month. Janet Ketter spread it all on the dining room table and let the people consume their own offerings.

The aura of celebrity seemed to blind and dazzle many of the visitors, and they approached Ketter uncertainly, their eyes cast down as if afraid to offend him by staring.

"You probably don't remember me," they would say, and to each, Ketter would reply, "Of course I remember you," whether he did or not. He had spent very little time in his hometown in the past twenty years, and in fact he remembered few of them, but one by one they reminded him of some relationship or incident that bound them, and Ketter nodded and smiled and shook their hands. He was

uncomfortable in crowds, even one that had come to
admire him, but he struggled manfully with his duties
while his wife took charge.

Bobby Hauck watched from a distance as Janet Ketter
worked the room. He could see that Pete's wife was used
to touting him. She took over automatically, although a
stranger in her husband's hometown, and acted as instant
master of ceremonies. To listen to her greet each new-
comer and acknowledge their little speeches of welcome
and congratulations, one would think that Ketter had just
finished a triumphal tour of the nation. The steady flow
of visitors into the house was not a ticker-tape parade, but
it was the best Janet Ketter had, and she made the most
of it.

"Quite a little woman," they would say to Ketter.

"You did all right," the men would add with a wink
and a nudge.

Ketter grinned wryly, as if with secret amusement,
basking in the adulation while at the same time feeling
embarrassed by it. Once in a while his eye would stray
across the room to catch Bobby's and the two would
break into smiles. As if they alone understood the com-
edy of it all.

Bobby watched from the edge of the crowd. He had no
need to mingle. He knew that before the day was over
someone would seek him out and draw him into a private
corner, swear him to secrecy, and divest himself of a
confidence. Bobby made his way toward Pete's son,
Michael, who stood by the window, his back to the visitors, staring out at the lawn.

In the yard next door to Ketter's house, a woman dragged
herself slowly across the lawn. She was weeding out dan-
delions with a trowel. Her legs lay inert on the ground
and she pulled herself with her arms, tugging her long
dress free from the dead weight of her lower body every
time she changed position. She was a woman of about

fifty, but to Michael Ketter she appeared ancient, as old and ravaged by time as a wicked witch in a fairy tale. Her hair was gray and unkempt and her face, unprotected from the harsh sun, was dark, dry, and deeply creased.

Michael watched with fascination as she slowly made her way toward the property line separating the two yards, a scruffy border of peony plants. She pulled a sack behind her, gradually stuffing it with dead dandelion plants. Michael thought of a snail, trailing slime.

She looked up once, her eyes meeting Michael's. She stared at him boldly, as if he, not she, were the freak. Michael jerked his head away, troubled by her boldness.

"That's Ellen."

Bobby Hauck stood next to Michael. After his initial statement, Bobby didn't speak, but joined Michael in his silent vigil, looking out the window. The boy was grateful for the silence. Conversing with adults embarrassed him. He understood that they knew much more about things than he did, but he also knew that they understood next to nothing of the depth of his perceptions. Most grown-ups approached him with an aggressive, probing attitude, demanding to know what he was thinking, what he liked, what he hoped to be. The men assumed he shared their interest in sports, speaking football and baseball to him as if they were masculine languages, universally comprehended. Inevitably they would mention their own children, compare his age to theirs, as if that mattered to Michael.

Bobby Hauck did none of this, and after a few moments of silence, Michael began to relax. Bobby Hauck, unlike most of the others, did not come to tell Michael what life was like when *he* was young.

Ellen, the crippled woman, worked close to the peony border, her head bobbing beneath the bushes as she dug with the trowel, then up again to stuff the dandelion in her sack. A jagged trail of brown earth stretched behind her like the prints of a small, sharp-hoofed animal.

Hauck tapped his finger on the windowpane and the woman looked up. Her weathered face broke into a smile as she recognized Bobby. The smile transformed her face, bringing instant warmth and a glow of kindness. To Michael, it seemed as if the wicked witch had suddenly metamorphosed into a mermaid, mysterious and enticing.

"She's my cousin," said Bobby.

"What's the matter with her?"

"She had polio, back when people still had it."

"She lives over there like that?"

Bobby chuckled. "Yes, she lives over there like that. She has crutches, she doesn't just crawl. And she lives alone. That's the way she wants it, she's very independent. She's also very sweet. Do you want to meet her?"

"No," Michael blurted. He waited for a reprimand, some sententious adult maxim that indicated how wrong he was to be shy, to be embarrassed. Instead, Bobby put his hand on the boy's shoulder and nodded once, as if he understood completely. Michael felt a sense of approval. Among adults, it was a rare feeling.

Edward Ketter had been waiting with increasing annoyance as his brother greeted well-wishers. He was not a man accustomed to being ignored, but he always had been good at hiding his true emotions. To cover his irritation he became even more hearty, ushering late arrivals to his brother like a fawning minister to the crown prince. He called his brother "the man of the hour" and smiled and laughed and waggled his head in admiration whenever anyone spoke to him. He listened to his friends and neighbors tell him of Peter's early days, of signs of courage and tenacity that they had divined when the brothers were still boys. Even then they knew, could sense, had a notion. Hindsight had made clairvoyants of them all. The fact that none of them mentioned any such portents of greatness for young Edward Ketter only served to increase his vexation. But still he patted backs, dipped his head as if listening intently, laughed aloud at the reminiscences featuring his brother. Edward Ketter was, above all else, a politician, and he knew the virtues of patience.

An elderly man had hold of Edward now, droning on garrulously about some exploit of young Pete's on the athletic field. Edward, who had been forced to watch all of his younger brother's heroics, suffering through one jealous hour after another of basketball games, football games, and track meets, knew that the old man's memories were as much in his own mind as in history. Peter Ketter had been a good athlete, solid and dependable, but not great. Cascade had produced no great men of any stripe—not until now, if one could believe the story Bobby Hauck had plastered across the front page of the newspaper. Bobby's account had been as much public relations as news, embroidering the basic news service facts with fluff and praise and a totally irrelevant history of Peter's accomplishments since grade school. Of course, Bobby and Peter had been friends since kindergarten, thick as thieves from the word go—an inseparable gang of two, even when their talents and proclivities would have seemed divergent enough to force them apart. Edward believed half of what was printed in the paper, but he had to admit a grudging respect for the television coverage. That, after all, was national. Thirty seconds on a prime-time newscast carried more weight, more proof of accomplishment and insurance of integrity than Bobby Hauck's blathering in ink for a solid year. If the networks proclaimed his brother a hero, Edward was forced to give it some credence.

He patted the old man's elbow.

"He's quite the boy, quite the boy," Edward muttered. He moved off from the old man as he felt his smile beginning to fade.

Ketter was alone at last and Edward advanced on him possessively, aware that all the eyes in the room would be on the brothers. He gripped Ketter by the neck and pretended to shake him, as if his affection was too great to contain: the proud brother, clutching his younger sibling to him. The grip on the neck gave Edward the appearance of dominance, suggesting that, like a parent, he was not only proud, but somehow responsible and still in control.

"How you holding up?" he asked.

"Tired," Ketter admitted. "My jaw hurts from all the smiling. I've never been real good at public relations."

"Well, enjoy it while it lasts. The prodigal son only gets to come home once . . . not that you're prodigal."

"I feel like a fraud. They all expect me to know them. Thank God I didn't have to announce their names."

"Just ask me, I know them all. They've always been my people." Edward moved his hand to Ketter's shoulder. It made them appear to be engaged in a very frank and fraternal conversation.

"Did you meet Frank Maust?"

"Frankie? Yes, I remember him. I never did like him. He's gotten fat."

"He's gotten rich, too. I suggest you start trying to like him."

Ketter sought out Frank Maust, a heavy man in an expensive suit, talking to a woman with long red hair.

"Who's the woman? I don't think I met her."

Edward laughed. "Stands out, doesn't she? Karen's the best-looking woman over twenty I've ever seen. In person, anyway."

"She looks all right," said Ketter. He forced himself to look away from her. She was the kind of woman it would be easy to stare at. And she carried herself with an assurance that suggested she wouldn't object.

"That's Frank's wife. Second wife."

"Why should I get to like Frank?"

"Because he's my biggest client. That makes him your biggest client, too."

Ketter looked again at the man who had suddenly become his biggest client. Karen Maust looked up and caught his eye and smiled. Unaccountably, Ketter felt himself blush.

Edward noted his brother's flustered reaction.

"She does have that effect," he said.

"What are you talking about?"

Edward thrust his tongue into his cheek. "Fair enough. Fair enough. You're a married man."

"So are you. Happily, too."

"Certainly am." All politicians were married men. Regardless of the facts.

"Where is Etta, by the way?"

"Not feeling well," said Edward. She was lying on the sofa, the last Edward had seen of her, a bottle clutched in her hand. Edward had not bothered to take away the bottle. He had long since ceased trying.

"Bobby did a good job with the house," said Edward. "He does good work at that kind of thing. He's got the patience for fine detail work."

"Bobby's a good man," said Ketter.

"That's what I'm saying. He wouldn't be my first choice to go along on a bear hunt, but never mind."

Edward looked pointedly across the room to the window where Bobby stood next to Michael. Their backs were to the room, their heads tilted slightly toward each other as if in secret conversation.

"Young Mike seems to take to him."

"People do."

"Some more than others."

"I've known Bobby since he was six, Ed. You're not going to tell me anything now that will surprise me."

"I wouldn't expect to, and I'm not trying. Just saying that Bobby has a lot of young friends. Looks like he's trying to make another."

"Let me worry about Michael."

"You've got nothing to worry about with that boy. Take it easy."

Ketter drew a deep breath. He had never been able to spend more than ten minutes with his brother without barbs being exchanged. Twenty years of separation had seemed to make little difference.

"We'll have to talk about the partnership soon," said Edward. "Find something for you to do."

"I have a law degree. I can do whatever needs doing."

"Little rusty though, after all this time."

"It won't take long to get the rust off."

"It's a pity we don't have many cases in your line," said Edward.

"What line?"

"The kind of thing that made you a hero. Makes me wonder why you quit, Pete. At the height of your career, so to speak."

"It was time."

"Wouldn't have thought so. National television coverage, the man who killed five of the ten most-wanted, whatever it was. Then all of a sudden I hear you quit the Bureau, and you're on your way home, and would I like to share office space with you? Well." Edward smiled broadly. He tapped his fist playfully against Ketter's shoulder. "What a great day that was for me. You can just imagine. Little brother's coming home, a hero, stepping right in to help me out."

"You don't need help. I never implied that."

"Well, I have it anyway. Only a fool would turn down a chance to get a man hot from national TV. You'll bring in customers who just want to get a look at you."

"I won't be wearing my horns. It might be a disappointment to them."

"Halo, Pete, not horns. You're the golden boy."

"I'd just like to get to work practicing the law and forget about this other nonsense."

"It may not be that easy, Pete. There's talk afoot of having you try for the county attorney's job."

"I'm no politician," said Ketter.

Edward smiled, not reacting to the contempt in his brother's voice, but noting it.

"I thought you were the power behind the party around here."

"I have some influence," admitted Edward. "A few favors owed."

"Then tell them to forget it."

"Don't be too quick, Pete. You want to be a lawyer, that means establishing a practice. And that means capitalizing on what you got. Right now you've got some fame. Use it."

"How about capitalizing on ability?"

"As a lawyer? You've got to prove that one. You don't have to prove you're famous. Give a speech and people will come listen. Take advantage, Pete. You didn't have to pay your dues by doing tax returns and chasing ambulances for twenty years. You didn't have to be a struggling attorney in a town that's got more than it needs. If you're coming into the firm, then bring something with you. Besides it's just a one-shot deal. Get out there and influence a few voters. Even if you lose, you'll be in people's minds."

"I'm not long on public charm."

"Hell, *I* know that, but nobody else around here does. So if you don't tell them, I won't. . . . At least think about it."

"I'll think about it."

"Good enough for now. In the meantime, I think we have a case for you to start with. Just your style."

"What is it?"

Edward Ketter smiled.

"A homicide."

Chapter 3

My father and I started "doing things together" with a dedication and intensity I found unsettling. I had become very used to my mother, and between us we had worked out a system for managing my maturation that allowed me great leeway for sloth and timidity. Because of the continual relocations over the years, she had become adept at making superficial friends, but very wary of relationships of a more durable nature. I became her close friend because I could not be wrenched away from her by the whim of the Bureau. I helped her with her card parties, setting up the collapsible card tables, filling the bowls with bridge mix and mixed nuts, slipping quietly through the smoky room and emptying ashtrays into a lidded silent butler. The women would coo in wonder at the spectacle of such a good boy and, per our unspoken agreement, I would politely respond as they grilled me with all the requisite adult questions.

In addition to these public displays, I was also an adept student at such niceties of etiquette as how to properly fold a napkin and how to set a table. My mother had absorbed from her mother a crystalline and inviolate way of doing things, as authoritarian and immutable as if inscribed in granite by an unseen hand. In her home in Columbus, etiquette took a certain form, style was acutely defined, behavior codified, and anyone anywhere else in life who did not follow the rules was, inarguably, wrong

*or tacky or worse. The world was divided into castes
according to how close one managed to hew my mother's
line, and the sad facts were that the rest of the world
never did quite measure up. New people were always a
disappointment to her, no matter how promisingly they
might begin, because eventually they would reveal the
baseness of their true nature by some solecism that might
go unnoticed by any observer with a less hawklike eye.
Unbeknownst to the person, he would slip a notch on my
mother's scale, and no amount of good works could ever
get it back. She inherited all these attitudes directly from
her mother, and the fact that she could not otherwise
abide her mother made no difference.*

*There were two exceptions to her rigorous grading sys-
tem. I was one, because I was still young and learning.
And my father was the other one. His gaffes were toler-
ated by special dispensation. He was her grand recla-
mation project. It was a lifelong job, but she was
determined to make him over in her own image. He took
it all good-naturedly, accepting those suggestions he
agreed with, tactfully ignoring the rest. Like a grand
Carrara marble, my father had within himself a solid core
of individuality, a sense of self, that would withstand any
amount of chipping and shaping from without.*

*In exchange for being her houseboy, confidant, and
companion, I was allowed a very loose rein in all matters
not dealing with surface manners. My mother had no
great interest in my "moral fiber." That area, long
neglected, became the specialty of my father, and he
began to exercise it with the zeal of an evangelist.*

*He was teaching me to drive the car and had taken me
to a deserted country road a few miles from our house.
(Cascade was of a size that all country roads lay only a
few miles from our house, and all of them, except for the
two-lane highway that bisected the town, were deserted
most of the time.)*

*I drove in spasms, unable to coordinate the clutch and
indifferent to the brake. We bucked and lurched our way*

in a route as meandering as a snake's. My father offered instructions in a strained but calm voice, reaching over to grab the wheel only when absolutely necessary. Ultimately my desire for calamity was too strong and we ended in a ditch. He drove the car out more easily than I had gotten it in, then suggested a break in the proceedings.

He seemed to regard my ineptness with more bafflement than anger. Physical things came easily to him and he could not understand why I labored so. I was embarrassed by my performance and felt weak and womanish.

We sat on the banks of a stream called the Little Muddy, next to a rusted iron bridge crossed with wooden planks that rattled alarmingly when a car passed over them.

"I used to come here," he said. He had taken to pointing out the scenes of his youth, speaking of them with a particularly somber tone, as if they were shrines.

"We'd fish. Or just horse around. We made a raft once. Five or six logs and some rope. It lasted about thirty seconds and I had to fish him out." I understood that "him" referred to Bobby Hauck. All of my father's childhood tales seemed to involve Bobby Hauck.

He chuckled, not really talking to me. "He was a terrible swimmer, he'd never put his head in the water, swam with it up like a dog."

He paused for a moment, then tossed a twig into the stream. It moved off quickly for a moment, then slipped into the shallows and slowly rotated. "This was a special place."

It was easy to see why it had been special. The banks of the stream were heavily wooded. Surrounded by a landscape flat and featureless, plowed field upon field broken only by a stretch of barbed-wire fence, the miniature forest that flanked the Little Muddy offered not only a change, but a release for the imagination. Here was a place where things could hide and surprises lurked. What was hard for me to imagine was my father as a boy. The

*whole idea seemed not only unlikely, but heretical. I was
not interested in an age when the gods were young. My
father was my father, fixed and immutable, and his
attempts to step out of his assigned role made me uneasy.*

"This was Pawnee Indian territory, as I understand it.
Nobody liked them, not the Sioux, the Otoe, the Crow,
the Blackfeet." He sounded as if the litany had impor-
tance. "They were cannibals, the Pawnee, which is why
they were hated. This doesn't mean much to you, does it,
Michael? Nowadays I guess it's invaders from outer space
or whatnot, but I grew up with cowboys and Indians.
Mostly Indians, as far as I was concerned. Silent hunt-
ers." His voice had taken on the solemn, introspective
tone he used for memorable confidences.

"I think that's one of the reasons I joined the Bureau.
The chance to be a silent hunter. That and justice. I
thought the Bureau would give me a chance to see to it
that things were ordered as they should be. There is an
order to the universe—not always easy to see, but it's
there—and I wanted to administer this order to man." He
snorted in a humorless laugh. "That was the idea, anyway."

He looked at me to see if I had understood, then tou-
sled my hair by way of forgiveness. He wanted very much
to impart something of himself to me, but I did not
understand what, nor how to take it.

"Were you scared?" I asked. "When you were under
the house, shooting those people, I mean. Is that why you
quit, because you got scared? That's what some of the
guys said at school: that you were scared."

"Fear's not important," he said. "You get used to it
and you go on to do what you have to anyway. Fear is
the least of it."

A rabbit appeared across the stream. In a gesture he
was probably not conscious of, my father lifted one finger
like the barrel of a gun. He didn't sight, didn't squeeze
the trigger, but I knew that in his mind—or in his

instincts—he had killed it. It was a reflex, devoid of malice.

"I want to learn to shoot," I said.

He looked at me, puzzled.

"You do it," I said. "You can."

"There's no pleasure in it," he said dully.

"I want to learn."

"There are things I'd rather have you learn."

"I'll learn them, too. I want to learn to shoot."

He fell silent, taking refuge in some private reserve in his mind where no one could reach him. It was a tactic that I never learned how to counter, and it drove my mother practically frantic. A woman who achieved her aims with the many thousand cuts of her continual speech, she was stymied by silence.

"I'm going to take a stab at this election business," he said finally, the previous topic subsumed and eliminated. "I'm going to run for county attorney in the primaries."

"I thought you didn't want to do it."

"Your mother thinks it's a good idea." He grinned playfully. "Your mother thinks I'm hot stuff. Don't want to disabuse her of that idea."

"What do you have to do?"

"Oh, not much, I wouldn't think. I'll be running against Walter Stimpf. Poor Walter's only qualification is he's got eight kids. That alone would seem to indicate a lack of prudence and self-control. I don't imagine I'll have to do much campaigning. I think the people will respond to integrity when they see it." Although I didn't realize it at the time, it was the first genuinely stupid thing I ever heard my father say.

"You won't have to do much," he continued, "but you will be expected to show up at the speeches and whatnot, so I want to talk to you about it before I make up my mind. What do you think, Mike? Can you behave yourself in public for a few weeks?" He grinned at me. I doubt that he had any conception of how much I loathed the

*prospect of appearing in a crowd, for any reason. The
agonies of adolescence had left him long ago.*

"I guess."

*"That's the spirit. I suppose I'll give it a try then: Ket-
ter for County Attorney." He fell silent again for a time
and when he spoke at last his voice sounded almost fearful.*

*"Sometimes," my father said, "I look on in amaze-
ment at the person I've become."*

The land was flat but not level. Like ice that had frozen
roughly, there were undulations in the stretch of prairie.
From the air, the appearance was of a landscape as smooth
and unruffled as a sheet of plywood, but from the road, as
Ketter drove, the minor swells and depressions gave the
impression of floating slowly across an untroubled sea, the
little ripples of land breaking the horizon only temporarily.
In spring the farms were as much mud as green and the dirt
roads that quartered the county like grids on a quilt were
alternately dust-dry and treacherously sodden as one drove
from high ground to depression.

The weather was erratic and extreme, regardless of the
season, and the spring was the worst. High winds, unbro-
ken by trees or landscape, swept the land, hurling dust
and grit into the eyes, and scouring the surfaces of build-
ings. It hurtled past fence posts and wire like breath
through a whistle, and the keening hum of myriad wind-
induced vibrations could be heard day and night. Early
settlers had been driven mad by the effects of the weather
and the isolation, and they had committed suicide by the
hundreds rather than listen one more day to the angry,
despairing whine of the wind.

Ketter sloughed his car through the mud at the base of
a small hill where tractors had gouged ruts that held the
rain. The Nyland house was a three-minute drive from
town, a fifteen-minute walk across the fields, twenty-five
by road, but a small hill blocked the town from view and

the vista in the other direction included nothing but plowed fields, buds of green struggling upward in even rows. Psychologically, it seemed as isolated as the middle of the Sahara.

Ketter got out of his car and stood for a moment, looking at the weathered farmhouse. He had been in Cascade for three days and his mind still raced with a mixture of remembrance and observation. He had returned as if to a foreign land and no detail was too small to inspire theory and speculation. Trying to square nostalgia with reality, he scrutinized his native land with the avidity of an anthropologist. They built their farmhouses with the back wall to the prevailing winds, he noted. The roads were unmarked, directions given in terms of the compass and the quarter sections. "Go to the section crossroads and turn north," they would say. A sense of the points of the compass was as necessary as to a sailor at sea.

This was not a working farm, he noted. There was no machinery in the yard, no animals in the feedlot. The land was worked by a neighbor who lived six miles away, and the house was rented out. No one named Nyland had lived there for at least twenty years, but it was still referred to as the Nyland place. In the public consciousness, this farm, like all the others, was not just property, it was an ancestral home.

Ketter realized with embarrassment that the woman was watching him from her window. He had been staring at the house, his mind adrift.

She made him wait on the porch as she moved around in the house. He could see her shape through the frosted pane in the door, approaching with annoying slowness, as if he were a salesman she wished to avoid.

"Mrs. Kiekafer?" He knocked again although he was certain she was making him wait on purpose. He had spoken to her the day before on the phone, and she treated him then with hostility, as if he were her prosecutor and not her defense attorney. A string of wind chimes dangling from the eaves of the porch roof jangled with irritating insistence.

When she came at last, her face was tight with resentment.

"You're Ketter?"

"That's right." He was surprised at her age. Ketter had expected a much younger woman, but she was close to his own age. Her hair was in two tight braids, with strands of gray and black that had eluded the plaiting frizzing up on top of her head.

"I don't need a lawyer, but I suppose you can come in."

"The court provides you with an attorney, Mrs. Kiekafer. It doesn't have to be me if we don't get along, but it has to be somebody." She stepped aside and Ketter walked into a room that smelled like a carton of books that has stood too long in a damp garage.

"I don't need a lawyer because I'm not guilty," she said, "but you'll do if I have to have one at all. Are you the one I saw on television?"

"Could be."

"I don't watch television very much."

"That's probably a good idea."

She smiled, her face so bitter it was almost a snarl. "Not for aesthetic reasons. I gave up aesthetic reasons ages ago. My set doesn't work very well."

She wore a floor-length peasant dress, faded and of an uncertain cleanness. A shawl was over her shoulders, but the scoop neck of the top revealed a chest of darkly freckled skin. The tops of her breasts sloped beneath the string tie of the top. She reminded Ketter of one of the flower children of the late sixties, the kind who came to maturity while seated at a potter's wheel.

"I hate people who say they don't watch television," she continued. "Everyone watches television. I can't stand hypocrisy."

She sank abruptly into a rocking chair next to the window. Her arms crossed over her chest in an attitude of defiance, forcing her breasts upward and accentuating her cleavage.

"Not very many people defend hypocrisy," Ketter said pleasantly. "At least not aloud."

She glared at him for a moment, then began to rock, pushing aggressively with both legs. Ketter realized suddenly that her anger sprang from fear.

"That wasn't my baby," she said. "There's no reason to say it was. They can't prove anything."

The body of an infant had been found in the farm's rubbish dump by the farmer who worked the Nyland place. The body was partially decomposed and the county coroner estimated the baby had been dead at least two weeks. It had been a newborn when it died.

"I'm here to see just what they can prove," said Ketter.

"Nothing," she repeated.

She turned away from him and looked out the window. Ketter could picture her there, alone in the musty house, rocking and staring out at the empty road. He felt a surge of pity for the woman.

Her given name was Sarah and her maiden name was Levy or Levin, no one seemed certain any longer. Whether or not she had ever actually married Kiekafer was also a topic of speculation, and Sarah never offered any information on the matter. Kiekafer had come from Cascade originally, a wild, strange boy who disappeared in the late sixties then reappeared several years later with Sarah in tow. They had lived in town for several months, Sarah trying to sell homemade metal jewelry for which there was no market in Cascade, and the Kiekafer boy doing nothing whatsoever that the citizenry could divine, except playing the cello every evening on his front porch. The cello concerts were as much an affront to the local proprieties as to the ear, and the couple eventually moved to the Nyland place, where he could play out his melodies to the empty air. Passersby would still give occasional reports of seeing the strange Kiekafer boy and his

Semitic woman, seated in the grass of the farmyard, the boy sawing away at the cello, the woman naked from the waist up, chanting. A bewildering and threatening anomaly, the pair of outsiders lived a life divorced from the town. In time the Kiekafer boy vanished. Clean-shaven and dressed in proper clothes, some said, gone to seek a job in a factory in the city. The woman lingered on, without friends, without family, living on God-knew-what.

"I can't pay you," she said. "I'm expecting money, but I don't have it yet."

"That's all right."

"The court pays you, right?"

"We're appointed by the court to take indigent cases. We do it in turn. There's a nominal fee."

"Indigent," she said. She closed her shawl over her chest. Ketter realized he had been staring at her flesh. "That's me, indigent. I had to sell my car to make bail. That was your brother's bright idea. Where is he, anyway? He is your brother, the other one?"

"Yes, he's my brother."

"I don't like him. He must be relieved you took me on. I think he was afraid my case wouldn't make him popular. He's a very popular man."

"Yes. People like him."

"You don't approve of me either, do you?"

Ketter hesitated. She was right, he did not approve of her. Seventeen years in the Bureau had taught him that most people were guilty of whatever they were accused of, but more than that, he disapproved of the general disorder of her life.

"I don't know you," he said.

"You don't have to approve of me. I haven't chosen my life. It just happened to me."

She turned away from the window and stood, dropping the shawl on the chair. Her bare arms were surprisingly muscular. She placed her hands on her hips and stared at Ketter, her expression defiant. Her breasts thrust forward, full and clearly naked beneath the dress. Her brown eyes still looked angry. Ketter sensed a wildness about her, as if it were all she could do to contain herself within her skin. She looked as if she could drop her decorum as easily as she had dropped the shawl.

"Well?" she demanded.

He realized that he had been staring again.

"Well, what?"

Her mouth fell into a tight, mocking smile.

"What are you gawking at?"

"I'm sorry. You reminded me of somebody. A girl I knew—sort of."

"You're a lot better-looking than your brother. But you're shy, aren't you?"

"Let's talk about your case, Mrs. Kiekafer."

"Are you a good lawyer, Mr. Ketter? I don't think I'll need one. I have powerful friends—I will be protected. Still, if I have a lawyer, I want him to be good. Are you a good one?"

Ketter paused. As he shifted his weight, he had the sensation that the rug squished moistly beneath his feet. He had an urge to rip off the curtains and let the sunlight pour into the room.

"I don't know."

"I thought you were a hero."

"For something else. This is my first case as a lawyer."

She laughed bitterly. "At least you're honest."

"Yes, I'm honest."

"But is honesty a good quality in a lawyer? I never would have thought so."

"I'm honest, Mrs. Kiekafer. Are you? Was that your child?"

She looked him directly in the eyes. It was, he knew, no test for veracity. All experienced liars looked people in the eye.

"It was not my child."

"When the sheriff took you to the courthouse, did you have a medical examination?"

"I wouldn't let them."

"Why not?"

"I don't have to let them, do I?"

"No."

"So I didn't."

"Mrs. Kiekafer, if a doctor did examine you, would he find that you've given birth in the last month?"

"Since he's not going to examine me, we'll never know."

"You realize I am your *defense* attorney, don't you? I'm not working for the sheriff."

"I'm poor, Mr. Ketter. I'm not stupid. I'm poor and I'm alone and, unlike your brother, I am not popular. I'm a single woman living alone in the middle of nowhere. I seem weird and exotic and 'forr-runn.' Any teenage girl with an illegitimate baby could have put that baby there. You wouldn't have to be a genius to figure out I'd get blamed for it."

She took his arm and moved him to the sofa. She sat beside him and curled one leg beneath her. Her fingers touched his upper arm as she talked.

"I don't have friends, I don't have family, I don't have money. I look like an easy target, but I do have some weapons. I know some people, after a fashion. And I know some law. There's no way they can prove I'm related to that baby without a blood test, and they can't take a blood test without my permission. That's self-incrimination. Isn't that right?"

She seemed to give off incredible heat. Ketter could feel the warmth of her whole body even though only her fingers were touching him. Her eyes bore into his. He felt uncomfortable, but found that he couldn't look away. When she breathed, her nostrils flared slightly. Ketter felt he was in the presence of something wild and sexual, a large animal coming into heat.

"What do you mean you know some people?"

"I know some people," she repeated, "after a fashion. They're afraid of me so they'll help. I count on them, but I don't need them because I have a defense, don't I? Don't I?"

Ketter realized her presence made him intensely nervous. His limbs were quivering as if he had just received a large jolt of adrenaline. He leaned forward for a moment and found his briefcase at his feet. He put the briefcase on his lap. She seemed to have moved closer.

"You should have someone with you now," he said, surprised to hear his voice was not shaking. "You must have family somewhere."

"If I had any family, I never would have let that son of a bitch bring me here in the first place. I would never have stayed."

Suddenly she was weeping, her lips trembling, her chin puckering into wrinkles. Small sobs jumped in her throat, like butterflies butting against the skin.

Ketter started to speak but could find no words.

She drew a long, shuddering breath that tore from her chest, and then burst into sobs. She dropped her face to his shoulder. He could smell her hair, a clean, soapy odor. He put his hand on her arm to comfort her and her flesh seemed to burn his hand. She moved into him and he could feel her body searing through his clothing.

"It's all right," he said. His voice cracked.

She lifted her face. Her eyes pulled him down. He dropped his mouth to hers.

As he closed his eyes, Ketter had a momentary vision of Marianne Fleming. Her mouth was set in the tight, embarrassed smile, but her eyes were wide, huge, inviting him in. Ketter opened his eyes. Sarah was returning his kiss with a wild urgency. His hand had found its way under the dress and onto her naked breast.

Ketter pulled himself away from her and moved unsteadily to the door. She was on him immediately, one hand around his neck. Her other hand touched him through his pants.

Her lips strained toward him but he opened the door and stepped out.

"Come tonight," she said. "You can park around back, no one will see your car."

He moved to the steps of the porch. The wind had risen to a howl and the chimes jangled crazily.

"Come, please come." Her voice was desperate. "If there's a light in the window, I'm alone!"

Ketter drove for half a mile then stopped, trying to calm himself. He had not kissed another woman since he got married. He had not realized he was going to kiss Sarah Kiekafer. He felt guilty, but he also felt strangely elated, like a schoolboy who has just gone further with a girl than he ever thought he could.

He looked out over plowed earth, shoots of green too low to be swayed by the wind. The view was dull and featureless but his mind was racing with conflicting emotions.

He looked behind him once, fearful that Sarah would have come after him, running down the road, but there was no one there. When another car passed, the driver looking curiously at Ketter, he drove off.

When night fell on the Nyland farm it was absolute. Black clouds billowed across the sky, blotting out the moon and stars. Lights from Cascade were blocked by the hill and there were no street lights in the country. Sarah had grown up in Philadelphia and had never known what true darkness was until she came to Nebraska, but in time she had grown accustomed to it and found a certain peace in being alone in her house, knowing that the light in her window was the only light for miles. Fear of the dark was atavistic, she thought. A tattered instinct left over from the times when dangers lurked in the blackness. There were no hungry animals in Nebraska, searching for her with glinting green eyes, only cattle and hogs, cats and dogs. Witches and goblins were creations of forest lands where men's imaginations cringed from the twisted shapes of trees, sighing darkly in the night wind. There were no trees here, no dragons, no monsters, no little people bent on mischief. The only creatures out at night were men and Sarah had no fear of them.

She often walked through her house without lights, saving on her electric bills while taking a certain pride in her independence.

She sat in her rocker, swaying gently, her face toward the road. Her hands still smelled faintly of the bread dough that was rising in the kitchen. She would knead it once more then bake it sometime in the middle of the night. She seldom went to bed much before dawn—she told herself it was because she enjoyed the night.

The television flickered in the corner of the room. She used it like a radio, seldom having it off day or night. The picture was very snowy, the reception terrible, but the audio was good and she listened to it all like background music. It provided her with a sense of company and she felt less alone when it was on.

Headlights came over the hill and turned into her driveway. Excited, Sarah turned off the light in the window and hurried to the back porch.

She arrived in time to see the car pull behind the barn, the brake lights turning the air red before going out. She turned on the back porch light so he could find his way to the house while she stepped back into the kitchen. She took off her shawl, then put it back on. She thought he might want to remove it himself. Better to show him too little than too much. Sarah understood the erotic power of the male imagination.

She heard his footsteps stop just outside the ring of light from the porch. She held her breath, afraid he would change his mind.

"Come in," she said softly.

His tread was heavy on the porch and, when he pushed open the door, Sarah was not really surprised that it was not the man she hoped for.

"What are you doing here?" she asked.

The man chuckled. A mean sound.

"I want to be alone tonight," she said.

"You never want to be alone."

"I do tonight. Go away."

He stood in the doorway. The nighttime smell of cool earth blew in.

"Go on. You made a mistake."

He stepped in and closed the door, then snapped off the porch light. The only light in the house came from the television in the next room.

"I want it."

"No."

She took a step back, not really frightened, but wary. He seemed calm, but very strange.

The man grabbed the shawl and yanked her toward him.

"I want it."

He pushed her to her knees and unzipped his pants.

"Get out of here!" she said, suddenly furious. She tried to get up, but he held her down by the braids of hair, jerking her head back.

"You son of a bitch!" She tried to claw his arm then stopped. He had a knife, which he pressed against her throat. Sarah understood that it was her own kitchen knife.

"I want it," he repeated. His voice had fallen very low.

Sarah reached into his pants and took him in her hand. He was soft and smelled of sweat. She took him in her mouth and heard him sigh.

She worked on him expertly for a few minutes, but when he failed to respond, she became annoyed. She had forgotten the knife.

"You've got to cooperate," she said, pulling away.

"You're not doing it right," he said.

"Why don't you show me how?" she said.

He yanked her to her feet by the hair, then pushed her onto the table, knocking the bread dough to the floor. Waving the knife in her face, he began to masturbate, angrily, furiously, trying to come on her.

The knife came to mean nothing to Sarah, a prop in a ludicrous farce, as impotent as the man himself. As his motions became more agitated, the knife jerked around erratically. Once he put it down to change hands. He was so pathetic, so comical, that Sarah could not help smiling.

He stopped at last, unfulfilled and panting with frustration.

"Forget it for tonight," she said, not unkindly. She felt sorry for him.

He looked at her face and smiled. His expression was suddenly one of great sweetness.

"You're right," he said.

He thrust the knife into her stomach.

The man kept a shovel in the trunk of his car for winter emergencies, and he used it to dig a hole in the plowed field. He buried Sarah with the corn.

Chapter 4

When it came to politics, my father was like a man raised within the church who lacks the faith. He understood the theology, but did not believe in the god. He knew that the essence of politics was expediency, that to be popular one had to blend with the changing background like a chameleon, offering one hope to one group of people, a different, contradictory hope to another. He understood that no position should ever be unequivocal and that integrity was only a pose. But he could not bring himself to act that way.

"They'll vote for me," he would say with a confident grin. "Look at the alternative."

His opponent, Walter Stimpf, was an attorney of no particular distinction who had fathered eight children by a very weary, washed-out woman who now stayed well in the background, as if the mere proximity of her husband would get her pregnant again. The wife and children, clustered around him like ornaments on a Christmas tree, were prominently featured in a brochure that Stimpf spread throughout the county. Bright and beamish, they fairly leaped off the page, radiant testimony to the potency and uprightness of their father. I had two of the Stimpfs in my school and wondered at the skill of the photographer who had managed to catch all eight while not one had a finger in his nose.

We spoke of Stimpf with mild contempt in our house, my father slipping into a parody of the cracker-barrel philosopher. "The man is as slippery as an elm branch," he would say. I could almost imagine the straw protruding from my father's mouth. He had taken to affecting colloquialisms of a bygone age while with the family, overplaying his role as yokel, as if in self-defense. Perhaps more of the world had rubbed off on him than he cared to admit, and he felt a bit uneasy in the mainstream of Cascade. Whatever the reason, he became positively sly and witty when discussing Stimpf, as if he imagined himself the young Abe Lincoln in debate with Stephen Douglas.

Stimpf had little personality of his own, relying instead on an ability to listen carefully before parroting what was just said to him. A conversation with Stimpf was reaffirmation of one's own ideas. "Like talking at a mirror," my father scoffed. "The man's a human echo." Which, of course, is a fairly accurate definition of the successful modern politician. Stimpf, while a private citizen, had offended no one and attracted little attention and few friends. Stimpf, as a politician, offended no one and attracted supporters.

My father, apparently confident of the drawing power of rectitude, continued to speak his mind as if the electorate actually cared what he thought about things.

If he was not skillful, he was dutiful. He attended every public function within the forty-mile radius of the county surrounding Cascade, shaking hands, speaking when encouraged, making a presence. My mother went with him every step of the way, smiling determinedly, offering encouragement, advice, and a particularly blindsided view of the campaign. My father had contempt only for his opponent—he respected the electorate. My mother had contempt for them all. No titled English lady attending a public function as a matter of noblesse oblige ever offered a more condescending manner than my mother. In her mind, my father was so far superior that the election was no more than a formality. You might have thought the election was really direct ascension to the House of Lords.

And yet, she tried. Give them both credit, they worked. And they had their supporters. Bobby Hauck was chief among them.

My father would descend from a lectern at the local fish fry or church bazaar or pancake breakfast—his face sweating, his eyes glazed with the kind of self-approval men get from listening to their own voice for a long period. The applause, polite at best, would fade quickly, and the background activity of eating or horseshoe pitching or socializing would immediately resume—and there would be his wife and Bobby Hauck, tireless in their support, unstinting in their endorsement. Bobby attended all the speeches and reported them. He ran editorials supporting my father again and again. He coached my father, without effect, on his heavy, labored speaking style. And when all else failed, he simply watched and smiled, with the same doting, uncritical eye of a parent whose child has a single line in the school play.

I was mortified. I wanted my father to win, because he wanted it, and because it would enhance my stature, but, more than victory, I just wanted it to stop. The endless public appearances embarrassed me. It was hard enough for me to make new friends without being related to a man who was constantly drawing attention to himself. It had been different when he was in the Bureau. His notoriety had been limited to the newspapers and he seldom had a case in the city we lived in. Also, I was younger and my friends didn't read the newspapers. Now, however, I was clearly, undeniably associated with a man who stood in front of crowds and spoke. *There had been a glamour to his work as an agent. There was nothing glamorous to a teenager about a man who declaimed like an unwelcome guest at fish fries.*

He asked me to help him just once. Flyers had been printed with his photograph (no undignified display of

dependents for my father) and his background informa-
tion. It was my job to put a flyer on every car's wind-
shield in the town shopping area, three blocks on Stone
Street, three blocks on Elm.

I made it down Stone Street, carefully putting my fa-
ther's likeness on the windshields of cars and pickups,
placing the wiper blade over them to keep them in place.
When I turned the corner onto Elm, I stuffed the remain-
ing flyers into the sewer. I did not know why, except that
along with the guilt it gave me a sense of vindictive plea-
sure.

If my father knew of this betrayal, he never mentioned
it, but he never asked me to help in the campaign again.

Meanwhile, he had lost his first client, a woman who
was accused of killing her baby. She had disappeared
before her trial and the assumption was that she had fled
because she was guilty. After a brief recital of the facts
of her disappearance during dinner one evening, he did
not mention the woman again.

Ketter spoke at a town picnic in the village of Dawson,
a hamlet of less than two hundred souls. Surrounded by
men in overalls and billed caps proclaiming "John
Deere" on the visors, Ketter spoke of integrity and justice. It was his favorite topic, and these sun-reddened men
and their wives seemed to him the perfect audience, for
it was a topic they too still believed in. This was not a
place for plea bargaining, not a moral climate that per-
mitted felons to walk the streets or shifty, dishonest lawyers to twist and abuse the protections of the law. When
Ketter spoke to farmers, he felt he was addressing the
very heart of America, a people, a consciousness that was
in direct contact with the most basic needs of life. Farm
life put a premium on common sense, the same common
sense that formed the rock-bottom foundation for Washington, Jefferson, and Lincoln—farmers all.

They were a patient audience, glad for the diversion. The men had rolled up their sleeves as a token to the relaxed occasion, and when they moved their arms, the protected white flesh of their biceps leaped like fish bellies against the brown sea of their forearms and faces. It was a scene Ketter remembered vividly from his youth, the startling white next to skin turned the color of drying earth by the sun. He smiled with the sense of comfort that things were the same. The audience misinterpreted it as an ill-timed attempt at friendliness, the disconnected smile of a politician who has been told to face the camera and look friendly but sincere.

When he had finished, Ketter lingered for questions. There were usually a few about his experience in the Bureau, and he had learned to turn the natural curiosity to his credit. A man named Bletcher, a farmer with the chunky build and thick neck of a football player, tilted his head toward Ketter.

"What about that smut business?" he demanded.

Ketter looked at him uncomprehendingly.

"I don't know what you mean."

"Frank Maust is supporting you, ain't he?"

"Frank Maust? I have his support, yes. What about it?"

"That's what I'm asking," said Bletcher. He seemed unaccountably angry to Ketter. "Is he paying for your campaign?"

Ketter's expenses had been paid by his brother, Edward, the money coming, Ketter had assumed, from contributions. The money involved was trifling and Ketter had given no thought to the ultimate source.

"Not that I know of. But I can't say for a fact that he hasn't made a contribution."

"If he's supporting you, he's made a contribution, you can bet on that."

Bletcher looked around to the others for confirmation. Heads nodded in agreement.

"I'm not going to argue the point with you because I don't know the facts."

"You're honest about that much anyway."

Ketter felt his jaw tighten with anger.

"What's your name?"

"Bletcher."

"Mr. Bletcher, are you suggesting that I'm not honest about something else? Because if you are, I wish you'd step up here and tell everyone about it and how you're going to prove it. That way we'll get it over with right now and not have to worry about any rumors."

He stared at Bletcher, willing the man to back down. Bletcher glared back, angry to begin with and now resentful that he was being put on the spot.

"I ain't saying you're not honest," Bletcher said at last. "I'm just saying what about the smut money behind you?"

"Why don't you explain exactly what you mean by smut money."

"Don't you know where Maust gets his money?" This from a woman, her tone incredulous.

"I don't know where you get yours, but I'd accept your contribution," Ketter said and immediately regretted it. Flippancy was not an attitude that went over well with the farmers. They spoke plainly and expected to be treated with equal candor.

"She gets her money from me," said another man. He seemed uncertain whether his wife had been insulted or not, but more than ready to defend her honor if necessary. "You want to ask me where I get mine?"

"You get yours from hard work," said Ketter quickly. "So do all of you, and I respect that. I assume the same about Frank Maust or any other man until I know otherwise."

"Maybe it's about time you inform yourself otherwise," said Bletcher.

"Maybe it is," said Ketter. "I tell you what, Mr. Bletcher, I'll look into this smut business, as you call it, as soon as I get home. That be quick enough for you?"

Bletcher shrugged and backed off a step, weary of his time in the spotlight.

Another woman asked Ketter about life in the Bureau and he responded gratefully, relieved to be back on familiar ground.

"It's a mail-order business," said Edward Ketter. His brother sat next to him and Etta sat in the backseat behind Ketter, her eyes fixed straight forward, her head wobbling just slightly. Edward drove with exaggerated care whenever his wife was in the car. To some he gave the appearance of a man transporting a delicate treasure, but in fact Etta had a tendency to be carsick when she had been drinking and Edward drove in deference to his seat covers.

"Nothing illegal about it. Just a mail-order business. Like any other." A quirk in state law allowed mail-order businesses to operate with enhanced profitability, and small conduit houses were sprinkled throughout the state, sending forth kitchen knives of magical durability, and record albums of the latest, greatest hits to purchasers throughout the nation. Products manufactured in New Jersey and touted on late-night television to sleepless viewers in New York City bore the zip code of corn country.

"What does he sell?" Ketter asked.

"Mail-order catalogue items. It's all very legal."

"Edward," said Etta, reaching to touch the seat in front of her. Her eyes gazed forward glassily and her voice was tight and apprehensive.

Edward pulled the car to the curb. Ketter helped Etta out of the car and she stood with one arm on the roof for support. She smiled vaguely in Ketter's direction, and he could smell the sweet, rich stink of fruit brandy. Edward came to her side and hovered, the fingers of one hand resting lightly on her shoulder.

"She just needs a little air," said Edward. He knew from long experience that they had stopped in time and Etta would be all right in a few minutes. Ketter wondered at his brother's solicitude after all these years. Time and experience seemed to have hardened him not at all to his wife's condition.

"Look over there," said Edward. His arm took in the broad sweep of downtown Stone Street. "I mean the youth center," he said. "Frank Maust built that for this town. The kids didn't have anything to do. You remember what that was like."

"I remember having hundreds of things to do," said Ketter.

"Yeah? Mostly work is what I remember. Work and boredom. How many times did you drive up and down Stone Street looking for something, *anything* exciting?"

"I did that," Ketter admitted. "But to tell you the truth, I remember it kind of fondly."

"Christ, you're in such a sentimental funk since you came back that you remember *everything* fondly."

"That's true."

"At least you admit it."

"But there's no reason not to. I was happy here, you were happy here. This is a town of happy kids, it's a great place to grow up. It wasn't all just cruising up and down Stone. I did a lot of other things, too. There was always a library full of books to read. . . ."

"Oh, for God's sake, Pete. Are you going to fight me on everything? Are you going to tell me kids don't need a youth center because they can go to the library?"

"So, he built a youth center. What's your point?"

"What's my point? My point is he started the committee and raised the money and put more than ten thousand of his own money into it. That's my point."

"What's in the center?"

"How the hell would I know? I don't have any children."

"You never even looked in there? What's he doing, selling dope to the kids?"

Etta Ketter lifted her hand from the car and settled it into the other one nestled across her abdomen. She turned her head slowly to one side, like a weather vane responding to a breeze, calm but inevitable. Her lips smiled slightly, but her eyes had a puzzled look.

"Christ!" said Edward, taking his wife by the elbow and leading her from the car. "Not on Stone Street, honey."

Etta's smile flattened and her lips stretched across her teeth, turning them into a taut, bloodless line. Her face had become pale. She looked at her husband quizzically, as if he had an explanation for her internal mysteries.

"Hang on, Etta," said Edward. "You're right in the middle of town now, hon. You don't want to do anything silly here."

Etta put a hand on Edward's arm, the fingers crooked rigidly.

"I'm fine, hon," she said. Her voice was tight and choked, as if it had not been used for a long time.

"That's right, you are. You're going to be just fine. All you need is to stand still for a bit."

"Um."

"That's right."

"What can I do?" Ketter asked.

"Just give us a little space here. Old Etta's going to pull through this one just fine, aren't you, Etta, that's right. It's just the motion that gets her."

"I know."

"But we aren't going to worry about old Etta, she's going to handle this one just fine." Edward's eyes never left her face, studying her as intently as a man watching a burning fuse.

Etta was breathing deeply, her nostrils distended. The skin where it flared was tinged pale green. Ketter moved away, walking toward the youth center, content to leave his brother to deal with the embarrassment by himself.

The youth center had been a dry goods store once, now long since outdated. Ketter remembered the front windows filled with bolts of cloth and strands of decorative lace. A dress had been standing there for years on a clothes dummy, headless, armless, with a metal pole for legs, only the bust and hips imparting any suggestion of a woman's form. The collar of the dress had been only partially finished, the needle and thread still sticking out of the cloth, a reminder to all the good housewives and seamstresses of work still to be done. The store had been hopelessly outmoded even in Ketter's day, a relic from a time when people still made their own clothes.

Now the front window had been blackened so passersby could not look in. Ketter entered into gloom. It was morning and he was the only human in the room, surrounded by banks of video games. A Ping-Pong table was in one corner, tight against the wall, proof that it was never used. The room seemed to Ketter to be possessed of the kind of sterility of an empty warehouse. He passed along the banks of machines, glancing at the names of the games, the lurid heroes and monsters and spaceships painted on the glass. At the back of the room he found a collapsible card table and on it a checkers set without checkers, a chess set with half the pieces missing, a deck of cards, their edges badly bent. He picked up the cards, riffled them against his thumb, judged them to be about three-quarters there.

Ketter scanned the room with a sense of distaste. Nothing available, nothing used that was not electronic. The room seemed hostile to Ketter, alien, as if designed for another species, and yet at the same time masculine. He could not imagine a girl spending time in the place, frantically working the buttons and joysticks on the machines.

"Old," he said aloud. Getting old. Automatic disapproval of the amusements of the young was a certain sign of age. Yet he did not fully believe it. His disapproval was grounded in something more than the difference between generations, he thought. Fighting an urge to rip the plugs from the wall sockets, Ketter left the youth center.

"They're not decadent, you know." Edward was holding the door as Etta demurely seated herself in the back again.

"I didn't say they were decadent."

"You sounded like it. Video games are the thing, it's as simple as that. We had pinball machines."

"That isn't all we had," said Ketter.

"Honest to God, Pete, you sound more and more like some kind of Puritan every day."

"How are you feeling, Etta?" Ketter asked.

"Oh, I'm fine, thank you," she said. She smiled brightly at Ketter, her attitude denying that anything had ever ailed her.

"It's just her stomach," said Edward.

"I know."

Edward got behind the steering wheel and carefully buckled his seat belt. He adjusted the seat a fraction of an inch, then slid the steering wheel into position. He turned his head toward his brother, waiting for him to put on his seat belt.

"It's like riding with somebody's grandmother," said Ketter.

"An ounce of prevention," said Edward. "You all set, honey?"

"Why, certainly," said Etta in the tone of a woman who could not understand what the fuss and solicitude could possibly be about.

"Only about three minutes further."

"I'm just fine, don't worry about me," said Etta.

Edward checked twice for traffic before pulling away from the curb.

"So what about the smut?" Ketter said when his brother had set the car once more carefully and meticulously on its way.

"Christ, Pete. You are tenacious."

"I've been called a lot worse. I was embarrassed, Ed. Those people in Dawson were looking at me like I was dirty. What is the smut business? Why do the farmers up there know about it and I don't?"

"Smut? Those people are living in the last century. I'm telling you, it's just mail order. He prints catalogues, offers items to people who want them. They send a check and he sends the item. Maybe that's too sophisticated for the farmers to understand."

"What kind of items?"

"It's a whole catalogue, Pete. I don't know what all's in there. Don't worry yourself about it."

Etta leaned forward, her head between the two men. Ketter could smell the alcohol, bitter now and turning sour. It smelled like fear.

"I could use something to settle my stomach, Eddie."

"Sure thing."

Obedient as a chauffeur, he pulled to the curb again. They were directly in front of the Angler's Club, a bar with a sportsman's motif, one of two lounges in Cascade. The procedure had a precise, rehearsed air about it. Etta let herself out of the car this time, scarcely concealing her haste.

"I'll be back for you in a little while, Etta," Edward called. Etta stopped by the entrance with a puzzled look, as if Edward had changed the routine. Ketter realized his brother had added the ad-lib for his benefit. Etta would probably be gone in the Angler's for hours.

"Why, that would be just fine, Eddie," she said. "I'm sure an hour is more than I'll need. Goodbye, Peter."

"Hope you feel better, Etta."

"I'm sure I will and thank you so much." Her smile was genuine now. It seemed almost indecent to look at her excitement. Edward pulled the car away so they would not have to watch her hurry into the bar.

They rode for a moment in silence but Ketter could tell by his brother's posture that his mood had already lightened. It was Etta, the sheer daily weight of Etta, that had driven the boy out of Edward.

"I'll want to go over to Maust's place today and see what he's selling," Ketter said.

"You're not the county attorney quite yet," said Edward.

"I didn't mean officially. Just so I know."

"And without Frankie's support, there's a good chance you won't be county attorney. You might remember that before you get on your high horse."

"Frank Maust has only one vote, as far as I know. Or am I wrong there?"

"You're wrong there. There's votes and there's votes."

"If I get elected, Ed, it's going to be because of one of two reasons. One, the people can see I'm the best man for the job, or, two, the people can see that Wallie Stimpf doesn't have all his batteries working. I suppose that they amount to the same conclusion. It won't be because of Frank Maust."

"You never liked Frank since you both were kids."

"You're right, I never did. Not that I ever paid him much attention."

"He remembers that."

"I doubt it."

"I just told you he did, Pete. Listen to me."

"What we thought or didn't think of each other as kids has nothing to do with anything now. We're adults. I'm more than willing to take him as he is now. I'm sure he's willing to do the same for me."

"What world are you living in, Pete? Is that really how everything worked in the FBI? Everything was done strictly on merit? I find that hard to believe."

"I find it hard to believe that Frank Maust is going to pay attention to any snub I may have given him twenty-five years ago. He's supporting me now, isn't he?"

"Sure. You're still a celebrity—and you're my brother. That's worth a lot more than you realize."

"I realize it. And I appreciate it."

Edward waved him away with an impatient jerk of the hand. "You don't begin to know."

A police car was waiting outside the Ketter law office. As they approached, Harry Killebrew unfolded his massive body from the front seat of the cruiser. A huge man, over six-and-a-half feet tall with wavy black hair, Killebrew had resembled the comic strip character Li'l Abner when younger. Ketter remembered him vividly from his youth, a gentle giant, the very epitome of the law's power coupled with mercy. The years had treated him poorly, and he was now fat and troubled with arthritis. He had been third-ranking man on the force of ten when Ketter was a teenager. After thirty years of service, he was now in command.

"Something you'll want to see," Killebrew said. He stood resting an arm atop the car, the door still open as if he had no intention of staying.

"Can it wait a few minutes, Harry?" Edward asked.

"Actually, it's for young Pete here."

Ketter grinned at the "young" appellation. To some people, maturity was not possible. Relations stayed in their fixed and immutable positions, frozen since puberty.

"Where do you want me, Harry?"

"In here's as good as any." Killebrew nodded toward the passenger seat. "Be sure to make it front seat though."

"Why's that, Harry?"

"Wouldn't do to be seen driving around in the back-seat of a cop car while you're running for office."

Ketter slid onto the seat, his knees next to a shotgun clipped to the dashboard. Harry Killebrew drove in direct

contrast to Edward Ketter. He seemed to pay no attention
to the road at all, his eyes roved the faces and scenery as
they passed and never seemed to look straight ahead, yet
he moved without swerve or correction.

"How's the campaign going?" Killebrew asked as they
drove past the town's city limits sign.

"I believe it's going very well, Harry. I've been doing
a lot of speaking, meeting a lot of people."

"I've been hearing."

"Hearing what?"

"Hearing all sides, Pete. That's my job, hearing all
sides of an issue."

"I didn't know my campaign was an issue."

"I saw your boy with Bobby Hauck."

"Yes?"

"At the paper, then just walking, talking."

"Bobby's a good friend of mine, Harry."

"Mine too. Everybody's friend, Bobby."

"I'm glad he's befriended my Mike. Bobby's good
with children, he's very natural with them."

"He's got a way with them, Bobby has."

"Why do I feel I have to explain this relationship,
Harry?"

"You tell me."

"I don't. I'm glad they're friendly."

"Ever take your boy hunting, Pete?"

Ketter realized they were on the road leading past the
Nyland house. He remembered his experience with Sarah
Kiekafer with a sudden excitement.

"Why?"

"Good thing for a man to spend time with his son,"
said Killebrew. He pulled the cruiser into the driveway of
the Nyland place, then past the weathered farmhouse and
toward the fields. Another police car waited in the middle
of the cornfield. Killebrew followed the first car's path
through the waist-high cornstalks.

"There's Bobby now," said Killebrew. "Amazing how
he always seems to know."

"It's his job to know things," said Ketter.

Killebrew stopped the car and looked directly at Ketter for the first time since the ride began. "Knowing things is everybody's job."

They got out and approached a tarpaulin-covered shape that lay next to a hole in the earth. Ketter took in the scene and understood quickly where he was, and why. There was a sickening familiarity about murder scenes.

Ketter looked at Bobby, trying not to let Killebrew's insinuations affect him. He greeted his friend warmly, laying his hand on the other man's shoulder. Playacting, he thought with distaste, ashamed of himself for feeling the need to do it.

"Dogs dug up the body," said Killebrew. "Neighbor who works this place found it. Rossiter. You know him?"

Ketter shook his head, keeping his eyes on the tarpaulin. He remembered the sweetness and warmth of her kiss, the touch of her nipple against his palm.

"We talked to him," Killebrew continued. "Not much help."

"Why am I here?" Ketter asked.

Killebrew nudged the tarpaulin off the body with his foot.

"She was your client, wasn't she?"

Ketter stared at the remains of Sarah Levy Kiekafer. It was no longer possible to see how she had excited lust in him.

"Thought you'd want to know, maybe identify the body officially."

"I can't identify that."

"No. Not a whole lot to work with. Thought you might help out there, too."

Ketter turned away from the body, his eyes taking in the details of the scene even as his mind told him it was much too late to find anything useful. Unless the killer had dropped his identification card at the scene of the crime, the trail would be a month old. He had worked on much older trails, but not for corpses.

"I quit that line of work, Harry."

"We don't have a whole lot of experience with murders here. We'd appreciate your assistance. Not going to be easy tracking down everyone who had a shot at that roundheels."

"What do you mean?"

Killebrew looked at Ketter with surprise.

"You didn't know?"

"Know what?"

"Sarah was the town whore, Pete," said Bobby Hauck.

Chapter 5

My father drove us to the bridge over the Little Muddy and pulled the car onto the shoulder. He had brought a lunch in a paper bag, sandwiches with slices of ham as thick as a pencil. He had cut the slices from a whole ham, trimming the fat and making a general fuss as if it were a banquet. Whenever my father began to talk too much, it was a sure sign of more camaraderie, and he had been talking nonstop since announcing our hunting trip.

He threw some peaches in with the sandwiches, letting me know that they were local fruit, which accounted for their scrawny, unfinished look but also for their unsurpassable flavor. Apart from reminding him to take paper napkins, my mother watched the invasion of her kitchen with a constrained silence.

On the way to the river we stopped at a grocery store, where my father bought a cold soda and a can of cold beer. Since he didn't drink beer, I was given to understand that the beer was for me.

"What your mother doesn't know won't hurt her," he said with a wink. It was hard for me to reconcile this man with the pillar of rectitude who spoke at political rallies with such ineptitude.

We went on our hunting trip without guns. The quarry, I feared, was me.

"How are things going with you and Bobby?" he asked
as we got out of the car.

"Fine."

"I look forward to the day you outgrow monosyllables," he said. *"Give me some details."*

"About what?"

"You and Bobby. About your relationship."

"Like what?"

"I don't know like what. You tell me."

We walked along the bank of the river until the road
receded from our sight and hearing.

"I don't know what to say."

"What do you two do together?"

"We talk."

"Just talk?"

"What's wrong with that?"

*"Nothing. I didn't say anything was wrong with anything. I'm just trying to have a conversation. . . . So, you
like Bobby?"*

"He's all right."

*"Help me out here, Mike. I'm trying to get a sense of
this thing."*

"What thing?"

"Your relationship with Bobby."

"Do you want me to stop seeing him?"

"No! . . . Do you want to stop seeing him?"

*"I don't care. I just see him when I run into him. He
doesn't act like an adult."*

"What's he act like?"

*"I don't know. I just mean he's not stuffy like adults.
. . . I don't mean you're stuffy, Dad."*

*"I'll accept stuffy. A little stuffiness between adult and
child is not bad."*

"I'm not a child."

*"I didn't mean you were. How does Bobby treat you?
Like a child?"*

"No."

"So how?"

"Like a friend. How does he treat you?"

"Like a friend," my father said. He laughed quietly, ironically, and shook his head. *"Like a good friend. We're both lucky to know him."* He picked up a fallen stick and threw it into the river. After a minute I did the same. The two sticks floated slowly downstream. His caught in an eddy and mine passed it. I waited for him to move, and when he did, I knew that he had digested something in his mind and was on to the next topic.

"What about the hunting?" I asked. We had walked a couple of hundred yards from the road. A field of soybeans was behind us. Through the trees, I could see the stalks of corn glistening on the other side of the river.

"Sit down," he said. We sat among the weeds fringing the field. The shade of the trees was within inches of my feet.

"What do you hear?"

"I don't hear anything."

"Close your eyes and sit absolutely still, then tell me what you hear," he said.

"I hear the river," I said, puzzled and annoyed.

"Keep listening."

We sat in silence for several minutes. I could sense his body seated next to mine, but it was a vague feeling, a perception of space being filled. I couldn't hear him at all. After a few moments, however, I began to hear everything else.

A crow flew overhead, cawing, followed by a blue jay, squawking in outrage. Then other birds, less obtrusive, singing and chirping. A meadowlark sang in the far distance, and something less melodic cheeped nearby.

"Sparrow," my father said in a hushed tone.

A high-pitched trill sounded close at hand and my father identified it as a red-winged blackbird. I was astonished at the number of birds that seemed to be around. They sang in an intricate, contrapuntal chorus, interrupting and overlapping each other. After a while I could hear one call and another respond in the distance.

"What else?" my father asked.

"That's all. The river and the birds."

"Lie down."

I put my head back in the weeds. The sun struck me full in the face, making lights dance behind my eyelids.

A car passed on the road, the bridge rattled in protest. As it drove on, I realized it was a truck, the rumble of the engine a louder growl than an automobile's. A cloud crossed the sun and I could feel the difference on my face. A new chorus began to reach my ears. A cicada chirped from the tree line. Closer to my car the breeze rustled the weeds and behind them I could recognize the leaves of the soybeans slapping one another. A branch groaned slightly overhead. A loud, scolding chirring noise I did not recognize came from the treetops. It sounded like a bird, but different.

"Squirrel," my father whispered.

The sun was out again, full on my face, and I could hear a steady throbbing beat. I realized I was aware of the pulse in my forehead.

"One more," my father said.

I sank deeper within myself while at the same time my senses expanded outward, stretching until it seemed they encompassed everything within miles. I learned that I could shift my attention, first listening at one distance and ignoring all else, then changing the distance, like stations on a radio tuning in and out at will. I pulled my senses close and stopped breathing. Finally, I heard it.

"I hear you," I said, triumphantly.

My father laughed and I felt his hand on my shoulder.

"Now you've been hunting," he said.

He opened the lunch and we ate.

Frank Maust had gotten fat. Ketter remembered him as a teenager, lean with blond hair bleached nearly golden by chlorinated swimming-pool water—the Mausts had one of two private pools in town—and the kind of delicate features that made him appear almost pretty. There was nothing pretty about his character, however, and he had a reputation for being rich, spoiled, and petulant but too much of a coward to be dangerous to anyone but himself. He had driven a convertible that he contrived to destroy several times, each time to have it replaced by an indulgent father with a newer, more extravagant model. His parents seemed to be seldom at home, and young Maust was an early party giver, doling out his parents' liquor and cigarettes at an age when most of his contemporaries were in training and still struggling to make the varsity football team. Maust eschewed sports, neglected schoolwork, and lived on the fringe of high-school society, counting among his friends the few other dropouts and a handful of older boys who had already escaped the constraints of school and parents.

Ketter recalled that the moral atmosphere of Cascade had been such that Maust's wealth and license had earned him an outcast status. While impressed by riches, Ketter and his peers had not been seduced by them. There was no way to buy the prestige accorded an athlete, and no chance to purchase friends.

Time had changed Frank Maust, submerging his delicate features in a field of flesh so his face looked like that of a snowman with the nose and mouth applied as a childish afterthought. His blond hair had darkened into that ill-defined color known as "sandy."

But what his wealth could not do for him as a child, it had accomplished for him as an adult. He was popular and powerful, and he greeted Ketter at the doorway of his plant with the kind of confidence that only continual success can bring.

"It's a pleasure, Pete," he said warmly. He spoke in a restrained, low-pitched voice that had no need to overplay its sincerity. "I've been watching your campaign with interest, but thought I'd better give you plenty of slack. I didn't want to mix in too much. Didn't want to steal your thunder, so to say."

"Not much thunder going on," said Ketter. "Once in a while I bring out some snores from the back of the room, that's about all."

"Never met a modest politician before," said Maust. He smiled, a slight twisting of his lips that left his eyes unmoved. "Your brother is a bit more inclined to lay on the trumpets."

"I'm not a politician," said Ketter.

"I've heard that, too, but never mind. You're doing fine and everything's going to turn out all right."

Maust had not yet moved out of the entryway. Over his shoulder Ketter could see nothing but an empty corridor.

"I've heard a little bit about your operation, Frank. Some of the farmers around Dawson mentioned it."

"Bletcher, was it?"

"It doesn't matter who it was."

Maust smiled his humorless smile.

"Sounds like you're protecting the witness, Pete. Must be your FBI training. You were well trained, we all sure know that. Great record you had, Pete. Great record. But in a court of law a man gets to face his accusers."

"This isn't a court of law, Frank. I'm just trying to determine what they're talking about."

"They? I wouldn't make this sound like a groundswell of opinion, Pete. You got one disgruntled farmer . . ."

"There were others."

"Bletcher is what I heard. Howie Bletcher."

"I didn't say that."

"Doesn't matter. Let me tell you about Howie Bletcher, Pete. He had a daughter worked for me, a young thing, nineteen, twenty, name of Margaret. A nice kid but not too honest. I'm a respectable businessman, I've got to act responsibly. I had to let her go, Pete. I had to fire the girl. Bletcher's never forgiven me, you can understand that. Hell, I can understand that. A man's daughter, he's going to take her side, no matter what. I don't blame him, I'd probably do the same, but I sure

wouldn't put much credence in what he says. . . . How's
your son, Pete? Is he settling in good?''

"He's doing fine.''

"I see that he's spending time with Bobby Hauck.''

"He likes Bobby.''

"Hell, we all like Bobby. He's an asset to the community and a fine professional journalist. A fine one.''

"Yes, he is.''

"That's what I'm saying, Pete. . . . You know we
have a youth center in town now, in case you'd want to
send your son over there, have him meet a few friends
his own age.''

"I've seen the youth center. I understand it's your
project.''

"I can't take all the credit. I don't run it, of course, I
just helped raise some of the money. I figured it was the
least I could do. Cascade's been good to me, I like to
help out when I can.''

"I was hoping to get a look at your operation here,
Frank.''

"Just personal curiosity, is it?''

Ketter smiled. He felt his face twist into the same
humorless set as Maust's.

"Sort of a fact-finding mission.''

"What a good idea. That's the way you're going to
operate as county attorney, that's good, I like that. We
don't want a man who sits around and waits for trouble
to find him.''

"You want a man who goes out and stirs it up on his
own.''

Maust laughed, a dry gasp.

"Of course you're not really county attorney as yet.''

"So people keep pointing out to me. . . . Do you want
to show me how things work, Frank?''

"Come on in, Pete. I want you to meet my wife.''

He led Ketter into a large office decorated with money
if not taste. Gooseneck floor lamps seemed to be craning
forward from every corner, and the edges on all the fur-

niture were smoothly beveled. There were no right angles anywhere.

Karen Maust was on the telephone, speaking in a tone that struck Ketter as oddly seductive for a business call.

"Karen's my right-hand man, aren't you, honey? I couldn't do a thing without her. I doubt I could find my way in and out without Karen."

Karen turned to smile at Ketter, at the same time tossing her head to clear the long red hair from her face. She winked in an open conspiracy to humor her husband's exaggeration. She was at least fifteen years younger than Maust and Ketter thought, as he had on first seeing her, that she was too beautiful to be anywhere other than on a screen. She made him think of the young Rita Hayworth.

They passed into Maust's personal office, a huge room with an enormous mahogany table serving as a desk. Ketter was struck by the sterility of the room. It was immaculately clean and neat, with no sign of activity of any kind. It was hard to imagine anyone ever having conducted business there.

"This is where genius works," said Maust, attempting another laugh.

"I was interested in the working part of the plant."

"You suggesting that the boss doesn't work? Just teasing you, Pete. I know what you want to see and intend for you to see it, but this is a bad time. We're doing inventory right now and things are just a god-awful mess. You wouldn't be able to make head nor tails of it—hell, it's all I can do to make sense of it right now. Besides, it isn't fair to all the employees to come barging in on them when they're working so hard. Tell you what, the dust will have settled in another couple weeks. Why don't you come back after that and I'll personally take you through by the hand."

"The election will be over in two weeks," said Ketter.

"Is that right? Well, then, it will be your first official visit as county attorney, won't it?"

"I won't need to visit it as county attorney. No one suggests that there's anything illegal here, Frank."

"What are they suggesting?"

"That it's immoral."

"Well, hey, I'm here to tell you it's not immoral. It's mail order. And morality isn't any concern of a county attorney anyway."

"It is a concern of the candidate."

"As it should be. I'm glad to hear you say that, Pete. I never doubted it, that's why you've always had my solid backing, but still it's nice to hear you say it."

Maust had led him back to Karen Maust's outer office. "He's everything we'd hoped for, Karen," Maust said. "A man who believes what he says."

"I never doubted it," she said in her husky, seductive tone.

"I think it's time we got to know the Ketters better, don't you?"

She smiled slowly, fully, her eyes twinkling with amusement, letting the full force of her smile work before she spoke. "Let's have them over to eat," she said. Her eyes never left Ketter's face. "Would you like that?"

Ketter shifted uncomfortably. The strength of his response to this woman troubled him, made him feel guilty without first defining his sin.

"That'd be fine," he said.

"It will be," she agreed.

Back at his car, Ketter sat for a moment, struggling with himself. He had been manipulated by Maust and the impotence of his position—the lack of badge or gun or superior authority—left him frustrated and angry. More surprising to him was the strength of his reaction to Karen Maust. He had already acted rashly with the Kiekafer woman, kissing her, wanting her, recovering himself only with difficulty, and the belated discovery that he had acted that way with the town prostitute made him grow hot with shame. For twenty years of marriage he had been faithful

to his wife—more than faithful (or less) because he had
never been tempted. Now he realized that fidelity without
temptation was no great accomplishment. It was easy
enough to be a saint if one had no taste for sinning.

Ketter had always prided himself on his moral strength.
It had been a strong sense of morality that had directed
him to the Bureau in the first place, and a sense of ethical
fitness that had kept him at it, marching through the
thickets of crime and the swamps of corruption without
fear, because he trusted the impermeability of the moral
garment that cloaked him. Looking down for the first
time, he now saw that the garment was beginning to tear.
The seams were strained, the ties shredding.

Since losing her job at Maust's, Margaret Bletcher had
gone to work at the creamery. She spent her days among
vats of butter, checking temperatures on the huge tubs
where mechanical blades slowly stirred the cream. When
a batch was finished, it was her job to transfer the new
butter into paper barrels, ladling it in with a paddle the
size of an oar. When the vat was empty, she cleaned it,
hosing the stainless steel with live steam, then with water
so hot she felt it through the rubber gloves. It was not
particularly hard work for a girl who grew up on a farm,
but it was nothing like the job she had held at Maust's.
That was office work, poorly paid but respectable, a clear
step above farming or the creamery. Margaret blamed her
father for the loss of that job; it was his stupid moralizing
that had ruined it for her. He had been preaching at her
since she could remember, and it had done no good, and
now he'd taken to preaching at everyone she came in
contact with, too. It seemed he wanted to keep his little
girl clean and fresh, but Margaret had news for him. He
was a good three years too late. She hadn't been a virgin
since the age of fifteen and had no intention of pretending
she wanted to be one again—at least not to anyone except
her father.

On good days she walked halfway home, hiking forty-five minutes along the dirt roads to the section crossing, where her brother would pick her up on his way home from the granary. She preferred walking to waiting at the creamery and it was good to be out in the fresh air after seven hours of smelling steam and sour milk. She also knew how good she looked in the tight creamery uniform. If men saw her walking, the material stretched tight across her bust and bottom, the hem riding up her strong legs with every step, if they turned and looked or stopped to talk—well, that was better than waiting at the creamery, too. But if there were no men around, Margaret didn't mind that, either. There was a long stretch of road just outside the town limits where she was surrounded by empty fields and could see any cars coming from a mile away. It was there that she lighted her cigarettes and smoked in security, knowing she could recognize any car long before the occupant could tell she was smoking.

The Buick passed her on its way out of town and Margaret did not bother to hide the cigarette. She knew the driver and lifted a hand in greeting. The driver looked at her in his mirror and she smiled to herself. Men always looked and some of them seemed to think she couldn't tell. Men in general amused Margaret, or at least she acted as if they did. She felt that by acting as if all of their posturing were a joke, she would appear sophisticated.

The car slowed and then slackened until it was almost crawling. Margaret could practically see the man making up his mind. Finally it turned around, bumping off the shoulder on the narrow road, and came back toward her. As it slowed to a stop next to her, Margaret held the cigarette cupped in her hand by her side. She didn't think she had to throw it away, but there was no point in taking unnecessary chances. Once in a while older men turned peculiarly censorious.

"Hello, Margaret," the man said.

She nodded, smiling sardonically to let him know she knew very well what he was after.

"Hello."

"You remember me, don't you?"

"I guess I do." She tried not to give away her contempt in her voice. She wanted her eyes to do it. Margaret had been told that her eyes were her best feature and she worked at making them expressive.

"Can I give you a lift?"

He kept glancing down the road and in his mirror, as if fearful of what he might see.

"I don't know."

"It's a long walk to the section crossing."

"How do you know I'm going to the section crossing?"

"I know a lot about you," he said. Margaret didn't like the way he was looking at her. She wished older men didn't always try to act coy when they wanted her. Younger men made no attempt to hide their feelings and she liked the directness, even though she made them wait just to show respect. Older men invariably acted as if they were only concerned with her best interests.

"There's a half hour before your brother gets there," he said.

"So?"

"Maybe you'd like some company. A young girl like you shouldn't have to spend her time alone."

"You can give me a ride," she said. She didn't know why she said it, she didn't like him. But he was right, there was a half hour to kill. "But that's all."

"Of course that's all," he said.

He opened the door for her, which is something none of the younger men would have done, but his eyes never stopped dancing between the road and the mirror.

"We're alone, if that's what's worrying you," she said. She dropped her cigarette on the road after one last, defiant puff.

"Nothing's worrying me. There's nothing wrong with giving a young girl a lift, is there?"

He turned the car around a second time, leaving a trail of dust in his anxiety to get moving.

"So how've you been, Margaret? Is everything all right at the creamery?"

"If you like butter," she said.

He laughed with an unfriendly sound. Margaret wished he would look at her so she could see in her eyes how much she disapproved of him, but he kept studying the road.

"I've always been interested in you, Margaret. You know that, don't you?" He touched her lightly on the thigh, as if he didn't notice what he was doing, as if he were just making a point in the discussion, but Margaret was not fooled. He left his hand on the seat between them, just barely touching her now. It was the kind of sneakiness Margaret disapproved of in the older ones.

"I wasn't aware you had any interest in me at all," she said. "A man like you must have lots of things more interesting in his life than me."

"Not really," he said. He made a fuss about swerving to miss a bump and his hand moved against her leg, this time with the palm resting on the skin just below the short creamery uniform skirt. She didn't move his hand away, preferring to do it with a withering look, but he still had not glanced her way.

He pulled off the road onto a rutted trail that ended behind a corncrib. Margaret could no longer see the road.

"What are you doing?" she asked, although she knew perfectly well. She had already made up her mind she was not going to accommodate him. She did not like the sneakiness of his approach. Perhaps another time, in another way, but not today. That was her prerogative, no matter what the men seemed to think.

"Is this where you hide and watch me?"

"We can be alone here."

"What do we want to be alone for?"

He turned to her finally and tried to smile. She could see how nervous he was, and then she noticed that his fly was already open. He wore white Jockey shorts. She gave him a look of scorn, but he didn't seem to notice.

The man reached for her, grabbed her shoulders, and pulled her to him. He held her tightly against his chest and Margaret did not struggle. She had learned that there were times to put up a battle and times not to. She fought only when she had an easy avenue of escape. All of the men would wrestle, some would hit and strike her if she resisted, but they almost never chased her. She thought there was something about running after her that embarrassed them. Not that she ran that often.

"I want you to do what you did the other time," he said hoarsely.

"I don't remember what that was," she said, although she did. She wanted to make him say it.

"Yes, you do."

"No, I don't."

His hand was in her hair, gripping her.

"Come on," he said

"You come on," Margaret said, her voice muffled against his chest. "You calm down now."

She pulled away, pushing his arm down.

"Whoa now," she said. "You don't want to act that way."

"I'm sorry, Margaret. I'm really sorry."

"Okay," she said. She felt for the door handle behind her.

"I'm really sorry!"

"Well, that's all right." Margaret was becoming frightened. He seemed so urgent. "I ain't going to tell anyone."

She opened the door and started out but he grabbed her viciously by the hair and yanked her back into the car.

"Of course you're not going to tell anyone," he said. "Why are you thinking about that?"

"I wasn't thinking about it. You're hurting me."

"You mustn't think about telling anyone. What we do is private. I'm not going to tell your father."

Not likely, thought Margaret.

"I said I wasn't going to tell anyone. Now how about letting me go."

"I want you to do it," he said.

"You'll have to let go my hair so I can," she said. Margaret waited for his grip to loosen. She was going to hit him in the face and bolt out of the car as soon as he released her. And if he didn't let go of her hair, she was prepared to hit him in the balls. She didn't like to do that to a man, but she was scared. She'd never seen anyone act so desperate with her before.

She felt something sharp against her throat, cold and metallic. She let her body go slack. She wasn't going to fight him now. Just do it and get it over with and hope he wasn't as crazy as he was acting.

"You don't have to do that. I want to do it for you," she said.

"I know you do."

She reached into his pants. He was soft when she took him in her hand.

"Do it right," he said. Margaret vowed to herself to do it the best she ever had in her life. Then afterward she would get her father's shotgun and shoot this crazy son of a bitch. She could feel the point of the knife against her throat the whole time.

She worked hard. The car smelled of his sweat and the odors of the creamery. Margaret couldn't understand why a man who wanted it so much couldn't get hard.

"You got to help some," she said at last, annoyed.

The man pushed the knife through the back of her uniform and he felt Margaret's body shiver across his thighs. It was much easier the second time.

Chapter 6

My father took me to the water's edge and made me lie on my stomach. It was the second of our "hunting" outings, and still I had seen no sign of a gun. I was beginning to suspect that I never would.

"What do you see?" he asked.

The sunlight reflected off the water and made me squint.

"Water, sunlight, my reflection," I said, understanding the drill this time. His face was over my shoulder, breaking and forming as the water rippled. Twisted by the water's uneven surface, he looked larger than he was, his head stretching long and thin, like some kind of giant, or an alien. I could not make out his expression, but I knew it was benignly intense. He loved to instruct me.

"Keep looking."

For several moments, I saw nothing more and began to believe that this time he had made a mistake, that there was nothing to observe and nothing to learn. Suddenly a fish as long as my hand swam into view or, more accurately, simply appeared in my view. It seemed to be hovering, moving just enough to counter the current, like a hawk working a wind, and it might have been there the entire time I was looking. With a flick of its tail it disappeared, then just as suddenly darted back again.

"Perch," said my father. "It's mostly perch and sunfish of that size around here. What else?"

I continued to look, my eyes now treating the surface and its distracting images as if they weren't there. The water seemed filled with fish, most of them of the intermediate size, too small to catch but big enough to see easily. Like the first one, they hovered and darted, as errant and purposeless as dragonflies on the surface. What they were doing I could not imagine, beyond fighting the current, their noses all pointed upstream and parallel to each other, aligned like iron filings reacting to a magnet.

"There's more," my father said, as I had known there must be. My eyes sought out another level, and there it was, as dramatically visible as if brought suddenly into focus in a microscope. Much smaller fish, scarcely bigger than a pencil eraser, moved within the water in an entirely different pattern from that of the larger perch. They were browsing the rocks, nibbling at the tiny bits of algae that adhered to the surfaces. One of the rocks moved, then moved again, and I was startled to see it was a snail. And no sooner did I see the one move than I saw many of them, all creeping slowly, browsing the algae too, like the fish, their antennae thrusting forward and back.

"The whole bottom seems to be alive!" I said, amazed that I hadn't seen it before.

"Yes, I see it," said my father. I realized for the first time that he was looking with me, going through the same stages, but ahead of me. For the first time I understood why he took such pleasure in instructing me. For him it was a process of learning again something he had long ago discovered and only dimly remembered now. He was teaching himself as he taught me.

"But there's more," he said. He laid his hand on my shoulder as he wriggled into place beside me, his head next to mine, his face only inches above the water's surface. The sun had been heating my shirt and his hand pressed it against my skin like a hot compress.

I glanced at his face. He was looking intently into the water, trying to find whatever we were looking for before I did. The tension around his eyes relaxed and I knew that he had found it and was now waiting to lead me to it. I looked back into the water.

We had apparently disturbed a family of blue jays, and they were scolding us loudly, outraged by our presence, but I had not noticed them before now, so intense had been my concentration. I realized momentarily that there was another world around us, continuing on its way, and we were merely observing one of many, many universes. Worlds within worlds within worlds.

I saw the motion first, a twitch of the water within the water; one tiny movement out of synchrony with the flow of the larger body. It twitched again and it seemed as if the water had taken on boundaries. An animal had formed itself from the material around it, assuming the aqueous properties, but somehow containing them into a separate body: a body with a curved, horizontal tail like a lobster's; many legs as thin and featureless as sticks, whirring away as it propelled itself; a head of sorts, pointed and antennaed; and all of it visible only when it moved.

"Shrimp," said my father, "the bottom of the food chain. At least the bottom as far as we can see."

I reached my hand into the water to capture this incredible creature, and the entire world dissolved, shattered like a broken mirror. It took several minutes before the world reformed itself, but now my hand was a part of it, looking grotesquely large and unsuited to the water. The optical refraction made it look as if my hand jutted off at an angle from my arm, which was still above the surface. My fingers rested against a rock, curled and cupped, ready to pull upward. The shrimp returned, many of them, flailing the water with their legs when they wanted to move slowly, or squirting off at amazing speed with a swish of their tail when alarmed. Several of them hovered above my hand, then slowly descended to the rock and began to feed off the algae.

Something within the shrimp moved, a streamlike movement of matter, clear but somehow more turgid than the rest. A river moving in a lake sailing in an ocean. I was seeing the quivering heart and gut of this tiniest of animals. I eased my hand out of the water, no longer interested in catching the shrimp.

"What did you see?" my father asked.

"Everything," I said, amazed.

He smiled. "You can never see everything," he said. "The trick is to see what you're looking at. What were you looking at?"

For a moment I wondered if his eyesight was failing, if he hadn't seen the same marvels I had.

"I saw something—a fish or a shrimp or something— that was made out of water."

"If it was made out of water, how could you see it?"

"I could only see it when it moved," I said.

He seemed very pleased by my answer.

"That's good hunting," he said.

We ate sandwiches that he had made, peanut butter and dill pickles.

"My secret recipe," he said, smiling. "Not only good but good for you."

"When do I get to do the rest?" I asked.

"The rest of what?"

"Hunting. When do we use a gun? When will you teach me to shoot?"

His good humor vanished, replaced by disappointment and a kind of weariness that he exhibited only when I had let him down.

"Guns are the easy part," he said. "Shooting a gun is not important. Killing things is not hunting. I thought you understood that."

I had understood it. His lessons in seeing and hearing had not gone unattended. I was not stupid, merely young and determined.

"I want to learn to shoot," I insisted.

"Any idiot can do that."

"I want to."

He sighed heavily. I could feel the disapproval vibrating from him. The peanut butter turned very dry and clung to the roof of my mouth.

"Do you see that squirrel over there at the top of the tree?"

"Yes."

"Point your finger at it."

I pointed my finger at the squirrel, which lifted its head suddenly and looked around, as if alerted to danger.

"Now say bang," he said.

"Come on."

"Say bang!"

I said bang.

"Look at the squirrel and say bang," he said. He pushed my arm up again so my finger was pointing at the treetop.

"Bang."

"Now do it again, and this time curl your finger toward you as you say bang."

The squirrel skittered along the branch a few feet, then turned his back to me.

"Dad, this is silly."

His mouth had turned tight as he tried to control his anger. It seemed to me his reaction was out of proportion to anything I had done.

He pushed my arm up again.

"You don't need to sight along your arm, if your eyes are good, your finger will automatically point right at the target. Use both eyes, there's no advantage to closing one, and don't take too long, or your arm will start to shake. Say bang."

The tip of my finger covered the squirrel's head. I was surprised at how easily, reflexively my eye and the "gun" and the target had all fallen into the same straight line.

"Bang," I said.

"Did you hit it?"

"Yes."

"Then watch it fall. Watch it bounce off the branches on the way down. Listen to its body thud when it hits the ground. Notice how quiet everything gets for a moment. That's because all you can hear is the roar of the gun. Notice how all the birds fly away and everything that moves and lives is afraid of you."

I put my finger down. The squirrel climbed part way down the trunk of the tree.

"Now you know how to shoot," he said. He got to his feet, gathering the remnants of our lunch in one sweep of his hand. "You go skin your squirrel. I'm going back to the car."

I sat alone for a long moment, trying to overcome my anger before joining him. All I had asked for was what every other boy of my age in Cascade already had. I understood that, as always, he was thudding away at some moral lesson, trying to shape my character, to mold me, to form me into an acceptable copy of himself. And to a certain extent, he had succeeded. I felt foolish and crude for wanting the squirrel dead, but more than that I felt angry. I was proud that my father was different, that he wasn't like everyone else. I knew that what he was trying to offer me was in many ways richer and better than what I was seeking. But I wanted him to be different, not me. I wanted to be like everybody else. I wanted to be perfectly normal.

When I returned to the car, he would not let me drive but took us home himself. He didn't speak but whistled occasionally between his teeth.

The Maust home was set at the very edge of town, the spill of the huge, green front lawn touching the street, while the rest of the property jutted into the countryside, as if trying to escape the town. It was a ranch-style house, large and sprawling and the yard—Frank Maust referred to it as "the grounds"—seemed to have been designed to match the architecture's earth-hugging style: squat shrubs and junipers bordered the street and the driveway. A few trees had been planted when the house was built five years earlier and they stood in pathetic isolation, spindly and frail, supported by posts and wires. Ketter thought they looked bewildered.

Visitors to the Maust house were inevitably taken first to the swimming pool behind the house. It was still a badge of affluence in Cascade, a conspicuous luxury in a community where ostentation was not well received. Or it had not been well received when Ketter was a boy. He was no longer sure if others would share his sense of mild disdain for Maust's bad taste.

"Olympic size," Maust said as he swept an arm over the green water. "Do you swim, Janet?"

Janet Ketter put a hand to her bosom as if startled by an indecent suggestion. "I can," she said. "But I have little occasion to."

"Well, you don't need an occasion now. You come over anytime. The darn thing just sits there empty most of the time. I call it Lake Maust. Karen's the only one who uses the thing."

As if on cue, Karen Maust stepped out of the sliding glass doors, a towel in hand, patting at her hair. She was in a lemon-yellow bikini that seemed to be the only thing that kept her from bursting her skin. Ketter had never seen a body at once so lush and yet so slim. He thought again that he had never seen anyone who looked as incredible as Karen Maust anywhere but on a movie screen.

"I am sorry, it won't take me a minute to get dressed," she said. She approached Janet Ketter, her hand outstretched, the towel dangling at her side in her other hand.

"I get so little time at the pool because I work at the office that I just have to take a dip whenever I get a chance."

"Of course," said Janet Ketter. Her smile had grown very tight.

"And I do like the sun. Not too much, of course, because it's really not good for your skin. But just a little. For color." Her skin was lightly, evenly, faultlessly browned, like a perfectly toasted marshmallow.

She stands like an actress, Ketter thought. Her arms at her sides, relaxed, and totally unself-conscious. And yet what an unnatural posture. No one off the stage ever stood with her arms at her sides. He looked at his wife. Janet had both arms tightly crossed over her chest, as if hiding from comparison with her hostess. Maust had one hand in his pocket, the other holding a drink. Ketter himself was fidgeting, unable to find a position that felt natural. She was giving a performance, he thought. She had to be. And judging by her attention to Janet, it seemed to be directed solely toward her. Karen looked only at Ketter's wife, spoke only to her, her eyes never leaving Janet's face. And yet Ketter understood that the performance was aimed at him. Janet was a convenient prop, beside which Karen Maust would look even more remarkable.

Karen left them, walking away with unhurried deliberation. Ketter watched her buttocks undulate in their near-nakedness. What confidence, he thought. His mind briefly conjured an image of his own wife, her buttocks pale in the darkness of the bedroom. She seldom paraded naked before him, not from prudishness but from embarrassment. Like many women, she did not like her body. Karen Maust, it appeared, had no such reservations.

Ketter realized his wife was looking at him. He smiled at her, reached out, and took her arm. She looked furious but also frightened, and Ketter felt a sudden pang of sympathy for her. He pulled her next to him, put his arm around her waist, and squeezed.

Maust had followed his wife into the house and they were alone for a moment.

"She's probably stupid," Ketter said, laughing.

"Do you wish I looked like that?"

The nakedness of her appeal touched him.

"I want you to look just the way you look," he said. "I love you the way you are."

"Would you love me more if I looked like that?"

"*She* looks like that and look what good it did her. She's married to fat Frank."

Janet Ketter moved a step, pulling away from his arm.

"You will let me know if you want her, won't you?" she said icily.

"Janet, it's not my fault what she looks like."

"You're the one she's showing off for," she said. "Don't pretend you don't know that."

"She never even looked at me."

"So you noticed." She walked toward the house.

"Janet, I haven't done anything."

She stared at him for a moment as if seeing into his soul. Ketter was not used to having a guilty conscience. He held himself rigid, determined not to squirm under her scrutiny. When he tried to smile, he knew it looked phony.

Janet broke it off and stepped into the house, leaving Ketter alone. He had done nothing with Karen Maust, but he had wanted to, he still wanted to. Since his experience with Sarah Kiekafer, he could no longer swear that he would not do something in the future. But I did not return to Sarah Kiekafer, he reminded himself. I wanted to but I did not. I could have, no one would have known, but I did not. That counted, he thought. That had to count. But he was not reassured.

He looked out over the pool. At the end of a fringe of grass, there stretched a cornfield, the stalks now chest high, the tassels of silk forming and turning brown. In a few weeks Maust would have a harvester rumbling through his backyard, gathering the golden corn ears within yards of the pool. Would the driver of that harvester get to see Karen Maust sunbathing? Ketter wondered.

Ketter's brother, Edward, and his wife had been invited. Ketter thought Maust used them as a buffer, agilely sliding behind them whenever necessary. The women came and went, taking a tour of the house, returning for a few minutes, then gliding off to the kitchen. Etta drank continuously, but discreetly. Ketter saw none of the early morning eagerness he had witnessed before. She was a skillful drunk, covering herself well, and sinking by degrees into a placid silence rather than boisterousness. She acted the part of the lady well, never taking the lead but always seeming to be attentively present. Edward, for the most part, ignored her, looking up to check her progress only when she accepted another drink. Ketter wondered if there was some established signal that would tell his brother that a danger point had been reached, or if Etta would finally just collapse on the sofa in a demure but unconscious bundle. Whatever their routine, Edward was clearly accustomed to it. He seemed happy and at ease, and Ketter wondered if perhaps his brother didn't need a third party as a buffer as much as Maust.

They spoke of the inevitable topic in Cascade—the harvest. And they spoke of the second inescapable subject at any local gathering—the state's football team. They talked about national politics with the assurance of men in a homogeneous society, secure in the knowledge that no one would contradict them. They discussed state politics, disapproving of the stranglehold exercised by the state's one true city. When they came to local politics, Ketter could hear the rumble of machinery behind their tones. Power replaced theory and Edward and Maust took on the character of men who speak with the surety of control.

At dinner Karen Maust took over. She wore a peasant blouse with a scoop neck and bare shoulders, and it seemed to Ketter as if she shone forth like a bonfire at the end of the table. Etta had fallen into silence, smiling benignly but saying little as she toyed with the food on her plate. Janet, too, had become quiet, but Ketter sensed it was the silence of fury about to explode. She stared at

Karen Maust as if the younger woman were spreading venereal disease with every breath.

With the other women out by default, Karen kept up the conversation single-handedly. She directed herself primarily at Edward, flirting openly with him in the harmless way of a young woman with a favorite uncle. Maust seemed to enjoy the performance hugely, teasing Edward and chiding Karen without an ounce of sincerity. Edward reveled in it, acting the roué. Karen proceeded as if Ketter were not present. The few times he spoke, she looked at him politely but blankly, as if wondering exactly who he was and how he came to be at her dinner table.

Ketter found himself growing stupidly jealous, resenting the attention she was giving to both his brother and her husband. In the end he, too, lapsed into silence, fearing that to speak would be to betray himself.

As they said their goodbyes, there was a sudden effusion of good feeling that often accompanies farewells. Unwilling to speak anything but niceties the whole evening, Janet suddenly began to chat cozily with Maust and Edward. Ketter found himself joining in, having a good time at last, wondering why he hadn't had more to say earlier. In the whirl and confusion of departure, he was suddenly face to face with Karen Maust for the first time. Her hand was in his and it felt as if he had gripped a burning torch.

"Thank you." He stared, feeling his tongue grow thick.

She looked deeply into his eyes, her own eyes flashing with that same amusement he remembered from the office.

He did not know if he managed to say anything further, or if she said anything to him, but it seemed later as if they had communicated deeply, as if she had sent him a message so open and eager—so demanding—that he had no choice but to respond.

That night he made love passionately to his wife. She knew why he was reacting with unusual zest and imagination, but pretended it was for her.

* * *

Frank Maust lay on his bed, the remote control for his
video tape recorder in his hand. A pornographic film was
on the television set but he watched it idly, paying little
attention as a youngish woman gyrated through a succes-
sion of positions with her male partner. Frank had drunk
too much at dinner and was feeling uncomfortable and
cranky. He was not able to drink the way he used to. Red
wine in particular seemed to give him a headache.

"I don't like him," he said, lifting his voice to carry
to his wife's dressing room.

"Who?"

"What?"

"Who don't you like, Frankie?"

He caught glimpses of her as she moved back and forth
past the doorway, the purple satin of her dressing gown
swishing lightly.

"Pete Ketter. I don't like him and I don't like his holier-than-thou attitude. I never liked him since he was a
kid. And I don't trust him."

"You've done very well with his brother."

"Ed is a different breed of cat."

"You're right there," she said, pausing for a moment
to look in at him.

"What do you mean?"

"I was agreeing with you, Frankie. Pete Ketter is a
very different breed of cat."

"Don't get any ideas, Karen."

She smiled at him, slowly, languidly.

"Do you like his wife?" she asked.

"She sure as hell doesn't like you."

"I thought we got on fine," said Karen, returning to
her dressing room.

"Whatever happened to women's intuition?" Maust
said. He rolled over to his side to see the screen better.
Another woman had entered the scene. She approached

the first, who was on her hands and knees. The new woman wore red panties and a halter.

"Come here," said Frank.

The two women were face to face. The camera no longer showed the man, although it was clear he was still behind the first woman. The two women looked at each other for a long moment, then their mouths opened and they kissed.

"I think I'm going to dump him," he said. He glanced at his wife as she entered from the dressing room. She slid the gown from her shoulders, revealing a powder-blue teddy and long, slender, beautifully tanned legs and arms.

"Who?"

"Ketter. I'm going to dump him."

Karen said nothing but stood by the bed, looking down at her husband. He glanced at the television screen. The first woman had removed the second woman's halter and was kissing her breast.

"So? You got anything to say about that?" he demanded.

"Why should I? Dump who you want. Why should I care?"

"He's dangerous, that guy. Stay away from him."

"All right." She still had not moved but stood beside the bed. Frank stretched out a bare foot and touched her thigh. He traced his big toe up toward the teddy.

"I don't mean to me. He's not dangerous to me. I'm perfectly legal. I mean he's dangerous to you."

She grinned at him, her voice mocking.

"I'm legal, too, Frankie."

"Don't be a wise ass. You know what I mean."

His toe nudged its way under the edge of the blue garment.

"You need a pedicure again," she said, but she did not move and did not remove his foot. "You want me to do it for you?"

"You know what I want you to do for me, and it's not a pedicure." He looked again at the screen. The second woman roughly pushed the first one onto her back and

stretched her body atop hers. The camera showed the
man, who was now seated in a chair at the foot of the
bed, stroking himself while he watched the women.

"Why would a guy let someone photograph him doing
that? How broke could you be?"

The camera returned to the women, who were now
working at each other with their tongues. Their postures
looked strained and uncomfortable as they accommodated
the camera, which continually zoomed in for out-of-focus
close-ups.

"Some men would pay to be in a situation like that,"
Karen said. She moved back a step and Maust's foot fell
of its own weight.

Maust was now engrossed in the action on the screen.

"You ever want to try something like that?" he asked,
not looking at her. "With another woman?"

"You've asked me that question before."

"Maybe I like your answer."

He rolled onto his back, still watching the screen. He
opened the front of his robe.

"Come on."

Karen let her teddy drop to the floor. She kept her eyes
on her husband to see if he looked at her at all.

"I mean what I said, Karen," he said as he felt her
touch him for the first time. "Stay away from Ketter."

The man on the screen entered the action again, pulling the head of one of the women to him. Grunting
angrily, Maust rewound the tape to the part he liked.

Bobby Hauck led Ketter into his office and closed the
door. The room was a terrible clutter with wooden trays
stacked six high on the desk, each spilling over with
paper. Long, yellow sheets of newscopy paper were
strewn across the desk in a pattern only the owner could
decipher.

"I thought you used computer terminals these days,"
Ketter said, trailing a finger across Bobby's ancient
upright Smith Corona.

"*The New York Times* uses computer terminals," said Bobby. "*The Washington Post* uses computer terminals. The *Omaha World-Herald* uses computer terminals. The *Cascade Journal* uses Bobby Hauck. And uses him and uses him."

Ketter lifted a spike with a circular base. A pile of papers as thick as Ketter's fist was skewered on the spike, each story edited in red pencil.

"This went out with the handpress, didn't it?" Ketter asked.

"The handpress went out? Why doesn't anybody tell me these things?" Bobby was rummaging through a bottom drawer. Massive, wooden, with doors that locked and stuck and warped in warm weather, the desk, like the equipment, was a relic from another age. It had belonged to Hauck's predecessor and the editor before him. Bobby kept it for sentimental value as much as utility. He claimed he could not work on metal.

"If you can't afford to be modern, go for quaint," said Bobby, pulling a folder from the drawer. "You should have told me you wanted to see this stuff," he continued. "I've been keeping a file since Maust started the business." Bobby put a hand on the file, holding it closed for a moment. "Remember, I've been doing this out of curiosity and a newspaperman's natural interest in developments concerning his community. There's nothing illegal about any of this. The existence of this file does not imply any sort of investigation or anything like that."

"Everyone keeps insisting it's all legal," said Ketter. "It's enough to make you wonder."

"A lot of things happen that I don't approve of personally," said Bobby, his hand still on the folder. "That doesn't mean I condemn them."

"I understand." Ketter started to open the file but Bobby kept his hand on it.

"And there's nothing in here you couldn't have found by yourself in due course. It's all available through published magazines and journals."

"Bobby, are you afraid I'm going to tell Frank where I've seen this?"

"I don't think there's any need to tell Frank anything," Bobby said. "This happens to be his line of work. Most people don't know about it in quite this much detail, but again this is not privileged knowledge."

"Let me rephrase the question. Are you afraid of Frank Maust, period?"

Bobby perched on the edge of the desk, negligently pushing papers aside to clear a space.

"Pete, I run a pretty good paper here. It serves the community. I do a better job than most would under these circumstances."

"I agree, you do great work."

"I'm not fishing for compliments. I'm just putting things into perspective. I know a lot of things about Cascade that I don't print. I'm not Woodward and Bernstein. In a town this size, an exposé would just mean exposing yourself."

"Do I interpret this as meaning, yes, you're afraid of Frank Maust?"

"Do you remember what high school was like, Pete?"

"You're awfully evasive tonight."

"Think about high school for a moment. Were you ever afraid of anything?"

Ketter looked at his friend's concerned face and realized he could not dismiss the question out of hand.

"Not that I remember."

"Of course not. You were strong. You were an athlete. You did what all the others wanted to do, but you did it better. That was high school for you. That wasn't what it was like for me. I was weak, I still am. I wasn't an athlete. I was . . . I was different, Pete. I still am different."

"You were more sensitive than most."

"We know what sensitive means, don't we?"

"Bobby, until you tell me what it means, I'm going to assume it means sensitive."

Hauck crossed his legs and leaned back on the desk, his fingers laced over his knee. It was a somewhat flirtatious pose, Ketter thought.

"Pete, I never knew why you put up with me."

"Are you kidding? You were my friend. Why did you put up with me?"

"You were my friend, but it's not hard to put up with the best athlete, who is also very smart and easily the best-looking boy in school."

Ketter felt his ears grow warm with embarrassment.

"I was that hot an item, was I? I wish someone had told me, I could have taken advantage of it."

"You did all right, as I recall. You never had much trouble getting a date."

"What does any of this have to do with Frank Maust?"

"What I started to say was that in high school there were a lot of people who found me offensive, or not to their taste, or just easy to pick on. A lot of boys become bullies at that age, and they spend the rest of their lives looking for someone who doesn't look and act the way they do. I was all right, Pete. I made it through all right because of you, because I could travel in your company, because some of that super-probity of yours extended beyond you and shielded me."

"Bobby, I honestly don't remember things the way you do."

"The point is, I knew where the power was. Cascade is a little like a permanent high school. The society here runs on much the same line and isn't much more tolerant of deviation than when we were teenagers. I know where the power is now. I have to."

"All right, I get the point. I'm not sure I like being lumped with Frank Maust. And I guess I didn't realize our friendship was based on power."

"Oh, no, Pete. You just happened to be powerful. That was a bonus for me. But I was your friend because I loved you. I still do."

The word *love* embarrassed them both. Bobby got off the desk and left the room, leaving Ketter alone with the file. Resolving to think about the substance of Bobby's confession later, Ketter opened the file and entered the world of the sexually desperate.

Maust's mail-order brochures offered sexual paraphernalia of every conceivable description from "French" lingerie to chains and studded collars. There were color photos of many of the items, including lifelike dildos of superhuman proportions, inflatable women dolls, vibrators in every conceivable shape, handcuffs, rubber suits, implements of torture. For some of the more exotic items, Ketter could only guess at their uses. There were pornographic books and magazines offered for sale, films and tape cassettes, their "plots" synopsized in exclamatory prose.

The file also contained clippings of the magazines where Maust's ads were printed.

"Who in hell wants this stuff?" Ketter demanded when Bobby returned to the office.

"You should have been a monk, Pete."

"I mean, I know it exists, I know there are a lot of weird people, but Jesus."

"Sex is important to a lot of people, Pete, desperately important."

"I'm not sexless, you know, Bobby."

"No, but you are prudish."

Ketter riffled through the file again.

"Yes, I admit to that. This stuff offends me."

"Some people have no other way."

Ketter looked sharply at his friend, wondering if he were describing himself. He considered Bobby Hauck his best friend in the world, he would have done practically anything for him—and yet he realized now how very little he really knew about him.

The brochure fell open to a picture of a young woman dressed in leather, a sneer on her face. She brandished a whip in one hand and a terrified, half-naked man knelt before her, cringing from the whip. The girl wore a military cap with a Nazi SS insignia over her long, blond hair and was supposed to look cruel, but there was something innocent about her features, some quality of wholesomeness that defied transformation despite the whip, the outfit, and the sneer. She looked to Ketter like a farm girl who had just turned from her milking chores to don a Nazi uniform.

"Who comes up with this stuff?"

"The preferences, or the material?"

"The material."

"Maust doesn't make any of the items he sells. He just distributes them."

"How about the brochure? Does he do that himself?"

"I'm not sure."

"Would he use any local people in it?"

"I doubt it. There would be too much of a stink if he did."

"Why isn't there a stink, anyway? Do people know what he's selling?"

"Sort of. The farmers in Dawson seem to know, you found that out. Most of the people would rather look the other way."

"Frankly, I don't understand that."

"Maust employs one hundred and fifty people at his place, Pete. One hundred and fifty. Assume each of them has an average family of four. That's six hundred people depending on paychecks from Frank Maust. The population of Cascade is just over five thousand. That means about twelve percent of our population takes money directly from Frank Maust."

"I had no idea."

Bobby seemed amused. "We have as many people in this community dependent on Frank Maust's sexual aids as on the corn crop. And the demand for sex is steadier. Not too many men go to sleep at night dreaming of corncobs. If they did, Frank would sell them."

"You find this funny, Bobby?"

"Ironic, but real. I respect reality, Pete."

"I love this town."

"So does Frank. Maybe more. He never left."

"Whose side are you on?"

Hauck replaced the file in the bottom drawer and locked the drawer.

"There is no need to take sides, Pete. I'm for tolerance. So are you, I think. At least you will be when you think about it. The stuff is legal, it harms no one. Agriculture is dying, we need the cash. That may be oversimplifying the issue, but it states it fairly well. You're shocked because this material offends you. But you've always operated on a moral code of your own, Pete. You never seem to have been tempted by mortal frailties."

"I've been tempted."

"But have you ever fallen?"

Ketter stirred uneasily and looked away, unable to meet Hauck's inquiring gaze. His conscience was already guilty in anticipation, he realized. He hated the feeling.

"I've got a fifteen-year-old son. I don't want him to grow up thinking this is the kind of world we live in."

"But it *is* the kind of world we live in, Pete."

"I don't accept that."

"That doesn't change the facts. I wouldn't worry about Mike. He can take care of himself."

"But I *do* worry about Mike," Ketter said heatedly. "It's my job to worry about him, he's my responsibility."

"Of course it is. I just meant, I don't think it's going to hurt him any."

"I don't want to pull rank on you, Bobby, but I think I know more about being a parent than you do."

Ketter was surprised at the sharpness in his tone, and he could see Hauck pull back, stung. The fact was, Ketter was not at all sure he knew anything about being a parent. He was trying his best and seemed to be losing the battle.

"What do you plan to do?" Bobby asked finally, after the moment of tension between them had stretched to the point of pain.

"There's not much I can do," said Ketter. "I'm going to tell Ed that I don't want Maust's support."

"Oh, Pete, no."

"It probably won't make any difference to anyone but me, but I don't want to think his dollars are paying for anything. . . . I don't want anybody else to think I have that fat sleaze working for me."

"There are only two weeks left before the election. Just let it go. You don't have to go out of your way to make enemies, you'll get plenty soon enough in the natural course of events. Just ignore Maust—don't antagonize him."

"Bobby, you don't get very many chances to choose what happens to you. Things are going on all the time that you don't know anything about and they end up influencing your life. Well, this is a chance I have to control the influences on my life. I'd like to get elected on my own, because I deserve to be, not because the porno king is behind me."

"What if you don't get elected?"

Ketter snorted. "Why wouldn't I? Who's going to vote for Stimpf? I don't need Maust's support to beat Stimpf."

Bobby tossed his hands up. "You can't *change* anything, Pete. He's not doing anything wrong. Whether you approve or not, like it or not, it's legal under the laws of the state and the nation."

"It's legal. I don't even say it's a bad law. I don't say I'd make it illegal if I could, because I wouldn't. There's a whole world of sleaze and bad taste and immorality and cheating and dishonesty and deception and unkindness and unfairness. People are bullies and snobs and slackers and cheats. I wouldn't outlaw any of them. But I don't have to approve of them and I don't have to associate with them. And, by God, I won't."

The phone rang, jarring them both. Bobby answered.

"Oh, no," he said, his brown eyes growing sad. He listened a moment more, then hung up.

"That was Harry Killebrew," he said. "He asked me to bring you, too."

Bobby was already out of the newspaper office and hurrying toward his car when Ketter caught up with him.

"What the hell happened?"

"They found another body," Bobby said. "In a corncrib."

Harry Killebrew sat on the hood of the police car. On either side of his dangling legs, the headlights shone on the corncrib. Two other police cars—the entire force of Cascade—were aligned next to Killebrew's, their lights on.

Killebrew seemed very weary, as if the hour was much too late for this type of work.

"Her name is Margaret Bletcher," Killebrew said.

Ketter looked away from the corncrib, surprised. Killebrew's features were hidden in the dark beyond the headlights. "Bletcher?"

"You know her?"

"I've heard about her."

"Well, a lot of us have heard about Margaret." The youngest of the policemen laughed and Killebrew swiped at him with the back of his hand.

"What does that mean?"

"Margaret had a reputation, if you know what I mean. Nice kid, I always thought. Just a little loose. Did you know her, Bobby?"

"I talked to her a few times."

"Old Bobby's talked to about everybody a few times, haven't you, Bobby?"

Bobby Hauck shielded his eyes from the headlights. After a moment he mustered a smile.

"I get around, Harry."

"I know you do. Did you ever give her a ride home out this way?"

"Sure. Once or twice."

"Is that significant?" Ketter asked. He disliked the condescension in Killebrew's voice.

"Hell, Pete, I don't know what's significant and what isn't, yet. Somebody gave her a ride out here and killed her would be my guess. The problem is, a lot of people gave Margaret Bletcher rides. I don't imagine more than one of them killed her."

Ketter looked down at the corpse. The dead girl's skin looked as pale as the moon under the headlights. The bloodstains on her uniform were as black as the night sky.

"Any idea how long she's been here?" Ketter asked. Deterioration of the flesh had begun rapidly in the warm weather and there was evidence of severe insect damage. He wondered at the lack of rat disfigurement.

"I can get it to the day, anyway," Killebrew said. He heaved himself off the car and approached Ketter. "Her father reported her missing six days ago. We figured she ran away or was shacked up somewhere, given her pre-dilections."

"Why did you want me, Harry? I don't need to see this."

"Thought you might have some insights here, Pete."

"I don't."

"Maybe offer a tip or two."

Ketter looked around at the scene. Bobby approached the body and looked down at Margaret Bletcher with no trace of revulsion. Ketter thought he showed the detachment of a professional. It was surprising in his friend, whom he would have expected to be more squeamish.

"You might seal the place off until you get a chance to check it out in the daylight. Although now that you've had three cars driving around here, I wouldn't hold out much hope for tire impressions."

"Plus it's rained twice in the last six days, plus this spot is used by every horny teenager within miles," said

Killebrew. "It's one of the few places they can get off the road and not be seen. I don't imagine tire treads are going to tell us too much."

"Well, there you go then, Harry. You've thought of it all."

"She was a sweet child," Bobby said to no one in particular.

"What are you mad at me about, Pete?" Killebrew asked.

"You're a cop, Harry. A cop who doesn't show respect to people is doing nobody any good and maybe some harm."

"Who? What did I say to you that wasn't respectful?"

"Not me."

Killebrew looked around, as if expecting to find a stranger who had wandered by.

"You mean Bobby?" he asked in a hushed tone. He took Ketter's arm and led him away from the corncrib into the darkness of the field. "I don't mean any disrespect to old Bobby. Hell, I've known him all his life. You too."

"What do you want from me, Harry?"

"I'm going to level with you, Pete. I'm lost here. This is way over my head. There's been one homicide in my whole career and that happened between two drunks who got into a fight. Now suddenly I got two of them. I've got no solid clues on Sarah Kiekafer and unless the killer dropped his wallet in the corncrib, I don't see what I'm going to get on this one. I'm not trained for this kind of work, Pete. I mean I've been to the FBI refresher school, they showed me how to use the computer and take fingerprints, but Christ, I'm a small-town cop."

"Call in the state police."

"I already have. Frankly, they aren't much good at this kind of thing, either."

"Nobody is, Harry."

"You are."

"I'm retired."

"Then just tell me what to look for. You boys can do things with fibers and sperm and all that."

"Do you have any sperm?"

"Well, no, I'm just saying."

"Fibers are overrated, Harry. All the microscope does is give you something to check your suspects against. First you need the suspect. And the way you get that is witnesses. The FBI doesn't solve crimes, Harry. We find informers. Then we find our suspect. *Then* we start checking against all the scientific data. First you have to have a warm body."

"Then help me find one."

"I told you, I gave up that kind of work."

"You live here! This is your community!"

"Sorry, Harry."

Ketter walked back toward the lights.

"I thought you were some kind of goddamned hero!" Killebrew said.

Ketter turned, the headlights shining on his back.

"You want advice, Harry? Cover the girl."

He got into the car and waited for Bobby. As they drove back to town Bobby asked, "Why won't you do it?"

"It's a long story."

"What happened, Pete? What made you quit?"

Ketter kept his eyes on the road. There was no place more deserted than a small town late at night, he thought. He liked the thought. Knowing that nothing was scurrying around while decent people were asleep. Except that something *was* scurrying around, he realized. Something deadly.

"I'll tell you about it sometime, Bobby," Ketter said. But he had no intention of ever doing so.

Chapter 7

My father remembered every storefront in town, every house, every lawn—I sometimes thought every twig and branch of every tree—and each seemed to speak to him with a resonance of memory that only he could hear. Sometimes we would take walks, setting out with no purpose—or at least no purpose that was ever made known to me—and just stroll until suddenly my father would stop and stare at a spot as if he saw a phantom there, waving its ghostly arms and demanding attention.

"This is where I fell off my bike when the dog chased me," he would say, his voice thick with import. He would look at a curb or bush or lawn so intently, his expression so bemused that I was certain he was reliving the moment. I felt it must have been a disappointment to him to come back to reality and to realize that I did not share what he had been feeling. I had not fallen off my bike there, no dog had chased me, and yet I felt a responsibility to try to experience what he was feeling.

He had delivered newspapers as a child, both on foot and on his bicycle, hurling them onto porches while pedaling past like some celluloid child in an old movie. It was difficult to imagine my father ever missing the porch and sailing the paper onto the roof or into the shrubbery the way they did in comic strips. He had covered three different routes at one time or another and had blanketed the town. In many cases he remembered who *had lived in the houses thirty years ago and if they had been kind to him at Christmas.*

Little had changed and that seemed to please him the most. It was easy to evoke memories when living in a time capsule.

"Continuity," he would say, putting a hand on my shoulder. "My grandfather lived in this town, my father lived in this town—your uncle Ed is living in the house we grew up in. I live here, and now my son lives here." I did not tell him that I was here only temporarily, that I had long since made plans to leave when I went to college and to put as much distance between the placid boredom of Cascade and myself as possible.

"There's a line through the generations. I didn't see that when I was your age," he continued. "And I wouldn't have cared if I did, any more than you care now."

"I care," I said dutifully.

He gave my comment as much attention as it deserved. "It becomes important as you grow older," he said. "I'd like to think that some of the factors that made me are also shaping you. Your values will form you, Mike. What you take in from the community around you, even when you don't think you're taking it in, those are the values you'll cling to all your life. You don't realize it now, but just walking these streets, knowing the people who live here, seeing the way they live, the way they think, the way they treat each other: these will determine in some measure who you become."

I didn't like the idea at all. It seemed presumptuous and indicated to me that my father didn't really know me if he thought any outside influences were going to shape me. I was my own person and would determine my own character and my own fortune. That much seemed perfectly clear.

Sometimes the walks would be more directly purposeful. He would take me to the scene of some bit of personal history and tell me about it in tones of import, as if relating the life of Thomas Jefferson. Inevitably on these direct walks, there would be a moral to his tale, some object lesson intended to strengthen my fiber or increase my understanding. When he was finished, however, he would always smile broadly. He appeared greatly amused for a time, as if laughing inwardly at himself.

"Parenthood breeds pomposity," he said once. "I'm not really such a stick. It's just that the responsibility of raising a child is so great, you hate to leave it to chance."

I found it hard to imagine that other parents were doing the same thing with their children. Certainly none of my friends ever mentioned it, although they all knew of my walks with my father. Everyone in town knew of them—recreational strolls were not a common practice— and after a time I doubt that there were few citizens left who had not been in the general vicinity when my father would stop walking and begin his reminiscences. I came to hate their understanding smiles.

"It's not that everyone in this town is good," my father said. "It's not that everything about life in Cascade is as it should be. The thing is that people are trying to be good. Given the choice, they would choose the best. That's the difference."

After he lost the election, the tone of my father's state-ments changed. They had not chosen the best, as he had been so convinced they would. They had chosen the cheap and flashy, the appeal to sentiment and emotion. As my father saw it, they had voted for a nincompoop with eight dependent children over a man of integrity, experience, and ability. He wandered the town after the election as if it had turned strange and he was no longer reflecting but trying to comprehend.

Only once did we venture into the newer section of town. The homes there had been built since his day, their lawns created out of cornfields, and they contained nei-ther magic nor mystery for him. On our single excursion there we passed the Maust house, the town's only real attempt at opulence. He stopped in front of the lawn, and for a moment I thought he was going to say something about it, but then I realized he was not looking at the house, but at a woman who had left the house and was walking toward her car. When she saw us she waved, then came down the long driveway toward us.

I had never seen a woman as undeniably gorgeous as Mrs. Maust. She wore red shorts and a man's white shirt tied in a knot across her midsection so that a large expanse of golden skin showed. The shirt was partially unbuttoned so that, although it did not actually reveal her breasts, it unleashed the viewer's imagination. She was completely decorous, given the season and the heat, yet at the same time wildly sexy.

As she approached I blushed just because of her proximity. I was certain that she could read my thoughts, that my lust was so obvious that she would slap my face or, worse, that my father would notice. In fact, she scarcely acknowledged me beyond a brief smile when my father introduced me. She looked at him, only at him, as if trying to devour him with her eyes.

They spoke of nothing, polite things, but there seemed to be an underlying weight to each phrase that only they understood. She laughed at something he said, her white teeth flashing against the perfect brown of her skin, and lightly touched his arm. Her fingers lingered for a moment on his flesh, and I would have given anything to have her touch me.

They did not talk long and we walked away as if nothing extraordinary had happened, but I felt as if I had been seared by a great heat. My face continued to burn for several minutes. My father fell silent.

"Did you know her when you were growing up?" I asked, unable to keep my mouth shut yet fearing I would betray the nature of my interest.

"Who?"

I could not believe he had forgotten her already. I did not consider him a sexual being, of course. He was my father, too good a man to lust for another woman, even if he was capable of lust, which I doubted. Still, from a purely aesthetic point of view, she must have made an impression.

"Her. Mrs. Maust."

"What about her?"

"Did you grow up with her? Here in town?"

"Not that I remember."

"Do you think she's pretty?" I persisted.

"Your mother's pretty," he said.

That, of course, was accepted dogma. Like every child, I presumed my mother was pretty.

"But she's not pretty in the same way, is she?"

"I don't know what you mean," he said. Which confirmed to me what I had suspected: adults in general, and my father in particular, had no interest in sex. Except, I thought, Mrs. Maust. She looked as if she knew about sex and was still intensely interested.

"Don't you think she's beautiful?"

"Mike, pretty is as pretty does. Your mother is pretty enough for me. I never really noticed anyone else."

As we neared a corner that would have put the Maust house out of sight, I sneaked one last glance and saw Mrs. Maust standing by her car, her hands on her hips. She was looking at us and grinning. I knew she knew about me.

Then my father did a surprising thing. He bent to tie his shoelace and, when he stood up, he looked directly back at Mrs. Maust. It was a clumsy ruse, childish in its lack of subtlety, and I was amazed.

Ketter drove west, aimlessly, merely pointing the nose of the car forward, allowing the highway to drag him toward the horizon. When he had driven far enough, when the turmoil in his heart and head had eased, he would turn the car around and let it find its way home again, like an old horse returning to the barn. Nothing would have been resolved by the drive, he would have reached no conclusions, but the internal fury would have passed, like a storm that had blown itself out. There would be another storm tomorrow, or the day after, but for the time being Ketter would have achieved a kind of temporary peace, a false serenity and acceptance that would allow him to go home, speak normally to his wife, listen to his son, act as if life and the world were not something that left him baffled and anguished by defeat.

Since the election loss he had taken the drives daily, leaving the office in the late afternoon and returning home by dinnertime. They seemed to be the only thing to help. Work provided no anodyne; it was undemanding and, since the election had diminished his notoriety, business had fallen off. Edward offered him the scraps, the house closings, the wills, all the petty daily work of a lawyer that offered no challenge but only steady sustenance.

"You've got to establish yourself," Edward said. "Develop a rapport with the little guys. Doing a standard will doesn't seem like much, I know, but it gives you a chance to build a relationship with the client. Let him know you're just like him. That was the problem. They didn't think you were like them. They thought you were— I don't know—otherworldly or something. All that talk about ethics. People don't want to know about ethics, Pete. They don't want to get riled up and take a jaunt on somebody else's high horse. They felt comfortable with Walter Stimpf because they knew he wasn't going to take them anywhere. At least not anywhere they didn't want to go. With you, who knows?"

"You make the public sound like nitwits," said Ketter.

"Not nitwits. They're not stupid. But they don't vote with their heads, either. That's what you don't understand. It's not a logical issue, and it's sure as hell not a moral one. They pick whoever makes them feel comfortable."

"Like Stimpf."

"Like Stimpf. Like me. Why do you think they've elected me mayor twice and are going to elect me county commissioner when I run for that? Not because they think I'm smarter than they are. People don't like someone who is smarter than they are, Pete. They don't like someone who is holier than they are. They like someone who smiles and slaps them on the back and tells them they're doing great and with his help, they'll do even greater."

Ketter shook his head. "Something happened. I don't know what, but something happened in the last week or two. I could feel it. They just didn't want to listen to me anymore."

"I warned you. I told you how to act."

"What happened, Ed? You're the expert. What happened?"

Edward Ketter busied himself at his desk, avoiding his brother's eyes.

"Nothing. It was a slow build. Nothing dramatic happened."

"Nothing dramatic. But something definitive. Like a whispering campaign that I couldn't quite hear. What, Ed?"

Edward Ketter lifted his head finally and looked directly into his brother's eyes. He smiled, his broad, automatic politician's smile, and his own eyes closed down from the inside, revealing nothing. He looked to Ketter like a candidate shaking hands in a receiving line, ever ready to slough off the present voter for the next one.

"Nothing happened, Pete. You lost. Don't worry about it. It's not your calling. Mrs. Stucker is coming in at two for our help in selling her house. Take care of her, would you? I have to be in court."

And so Ketter drove in the late afternoons, passing unseeing through fields so green they seemed to suck the sunlight from the sky. The harvesters were just beginning to take the corn, the giant machines growling down the rows, their snouts to the ground. The noise was unceasing and the drivers sat in their closed cabs, stereophones pressed to their ears, trying to keep out the tumult of the engines and the tearing husks and the flying ears of corn with the sounds of electric guitars and echo-chambered voices.

Ketter noticed little of it. Like a hurt animal, he pulled into himself, curling around the wound of public rejection. He avoided the public now, just as he had courted them only weeks before. Every trip outside his office, every drive down main street seemed to subject him to mocking eyes. He felt as if a chorus of voices followed him everywhere, chanting, ''We didn't want you. We didn't like you. We didn't take you.''

It was ridiculous, he knew. He had lost an election, not been dismissed from the human race. It was ludicrous to take it to heart, childish and insecure to think it meant anything personal. And yet it hurt. It pained and embittered him and forced him into himself.

The murmured comforts of his wife annoyed him. When she spoke out angrily, denouncing the electorate as fools and ingrates, he felt obliged to take the other side, speaking with sweet reason, and that only annoyed him more. He felt a need to be strong in front of his wife. If she took it badly, he felt obliged to take it well. Her emotionalism forced him into a stance of outward stoicism that he did not feel. He wanted, more than anything, to leave Cascade, to keep on driving on one of his afternoon journeys and not stop until he reached a place where there was real peace and acceptance. He knew he would not do that, and so he began slowly to allow himself to seek peace elsewhere. Or if not peace, then surcease. He began slowly to give himself permission to replace his pain with excitement. He began, on his afternoons of solitude, to think of Karen Maust.

Following her was not possible, not by accepted Bureau methods. Cascade was too small for adequate concealment; all cars were recognizable. He could hardly stroll down main street, pretending to window-shop, while Karen Maust wandered in and out of department stores. There were no department stores; shopping was not a leisure pastime in Cascade. He could not stake out her home or office.

So Ketter began to follow her from the front, interposing himself along her routes so their meetings appeared coincidental. If she was deceived, he could not tell, for she greeted him every time with the same knowing, slightly mocking attitude of amusement.

He met her at one of the town's two supermarkets, pretending to purchase produce he did not want. They talked idly, casually, as neighbors and acquaintances. There was nothing in their words to betray them in any way. The real message was passed through their eyes and through her teasing, tormenting smile. Ketter found it impossible to act naturally. His heart was pounding too loudly; he felt that she would see his lips quivering if he looked at her too long. He exhibited an unusual interest in the grapefruits and kohlrabies, selecting one, putting it back, selecting the same one a moment later and examining it all over again.

She seemed perfectly at ease, and he wondered how many times she had practiced flirtation—for he was sure she was responding to him, although he could not have said exactly how he knew.

Afterward, feeling as guilty of betrayal as if he had actually slept with her, Ketter would return home and make a surprising and inexplicable gift to his wife of cabbage and carrots.

"It's not that anything is happening," he said to Bobby Hauck as they sat alone in the alcoholic shadows of the Angler's Club. Ketter swirled a flat glass of beer that he had nursed for more than an hour. Bobby sipped his gin and tonic and nodded understandingly, waiting.

"I mean, I'm not going to let anything happen. I don't believe in it, for one thing. I don't approve of affairs, I don't approve of people who have them. It wouldn't be worth it. I value my self-esteem too much. I just wouldn't like myself much anymore if I let anything happen. You can understand that, can't you?''

Bobby inclined his head slightly, and Ketter read agreement into the motion.

"But, even so, I should stay away from her. That's the sensible thing to do. Christ, Bobby, she's the sexiest thing I've ever seen!''

Aware that he had raised his voice, Ketter looked around the room. In the late afternoon, they were virtually alone.

Ketter twisted the glass between both hands and studied the miniature whirlpool he had created.

"Just thinking about her, I get a reaction in my gut. If I see her coming, I swear to God my legs threaten to give out on me.''

"She is a beautiful woman,'' said Bobby, speaking into a silence.

"It's almost as if I were afraid of her. I mean, I know a lot about fear, Bobby, and that's what this is like. It's like . . . do you remember when you and I and Earl Gibson took that Tubock girl out and took turns screwing her? Remember that? That was my first time and I was scared to death until I actually did it.''

"She's married to a man in Auburn now,'' Bobby said. "A garage mechanic there. She has five kids.''

"That was your first time, too, wasn't it?''

"I didn't actually do it with her.''

"You didn't? You took your turn in the car with her.''

"Not actually,'' Bobby said. "I felt sorry for her. We talked until you and Earl came back.''

"Christ, for twenty-five years I thought you screwed her, too. Why didn't you tell me then?''

Bobby shrugged. "I didn't think you were quite ready for it then.''

"You were right. . . . What do you mean you felt sorry for her?''

"She was crying."

"Crying? I didn't know that."

"Well, you had other concerns. She told me she got used a lot by various guys, but that she really liked you. That's why she agreed to go."

"She really liked me?" Ketter could feel the effect on his ego, even two decades later. "I never knew that."

"You didn't know a lot of things."

"You make me feel like a hairy animal, Bobby. Like some kind of inconsiderate, insensitive beast."

"You're not, Pete. You're a good man, a good friend, but there are a lot of things you don't see."

"Like what?"

Bobby sipped his drink and stared for a moment over Ketter's shoulder. When he looked him in the face at last, he smiled.

"It's all sex, Pete. Even here in Cascade, even with you, no matter how much you'd like it to be different. It's hidden sex or it's open sex. It's straight sex or it's crooked sex, it's successful or it's frustrated, but it's all sex."

"I don't know what you're talking about."

"Well, you do and you don't. On some level you know, although it doesn't square with the way you want the world to be. You're not going to the supermarket just for vegetables, Pete. Whether or not anything has happened with Karen Maust, whether or not it will, it's still very much about sex. The same is true for us, for our relationship."

"What are you saying?"

"Just being honest for the first time in our lives."

Ketter rose quickly to his feet, scraping the chair noisily away.

"Are you trying to tell me! . . ." He stopped, his jaw trembling with anger, his fist tight. Then he breathed deeply and, with an effort, unballed his fist.

"I'm not going to hit you, Bobby," he said, seeing the fright in his friend's eyes.

"I'd fight back," Bobby said.

Ketter righted his chair and sat down once more.

"I'm glad to hear that."

"I'm not ashamed, Pete. You should know that, I'm not ashamed anymore. I was for the longest time, and very much afraid, too. But either I've outgrown the fear or the times have changed so much . . . I don't know. Don't misunderstand me, I'm in a very sensitive position in this community. I'm very vulnerable, and I'm not broadcasting anything to the general public, but I don't have to hide from my friend."

"Why are you telling me this now, Bobby?"

"Because you're telling me about yourself, maybe? Because you're letting me see inside you and you deserve no less of me? Maybe. Maybe because I'm jealous of Karen Maust."

Ketter sat in silence, unable to meet his friend's eyes, his gaze on the table. He made a meaningless design in the condensation that had dripped from his beer glass.

"This is a little awkward," he said at last.

"Yes."

"I guess I always knew."

"You knew. You just didn't want to admit it. Sex is always there, whether there is any touching or not."

"There won't be any touching between us, Bobby," Ketter said sternly.

Bobby grinned.

"I mean it."

"I know you do. But I'm not going to pretend I don't want to."

"So where does that leave us?"

"I think that's up to you. It's your move, Pete."

"Are we still friends?"

"As much as we ever were," said Bobby. "Maybe more."

Ketter fell silent again. The world seemed to have shifted once more on its axis, and once again things were twisted and distorted. North was no longer north but slightly skewed to the east, and everything else had to adjust accordingly.

"The times they are a-changin'," he said at last with a bitter chuckle.

"Yes, they are," Bobby agreed.

"I don't like it," said Ketter.

"They're changin' anyway," said Bobby.

Ketter dreamed of destruction, of a world that was collapsing, slowly, undramatically, folding under its own weight and crushing all within. In the heart of the world stood Ketter, sensing rather than seeing the immense pressure of a world falling inward. He held his arms out to withstand it, like Samson in the temple, blinded and betrayed, a giant under whose legs scurried an indifferent populace. "It's coming!" he yelled, but no one seemed to hear him. He realized he was holding the pillars of the earth in place for himself, not for them, they didn't care, only he cared. And yet he yelled again, "It's coming!" prompted by a sense of duty, but no longer certain to whom he owed the duty. The pillars moved under his hand and he realized they were smooth and soft and incredibly warm.

The pillars turned into a beautiful woman, one he had never seen before, but one so beautiful that he felt his arms weaken and his legs enfeebled. She moved sensuously, rubbing her abdomen against his palm, then slowly lowering herself until his hand touched her breasts. She opened her lips in ecstasy and began to shake. Ketter realized the world was about to collapse, that her shivers were the tremors of destruction, but he could not pull away from her, she held his hand fast against her breasts and she moved her lower body against his leg, pressing into him. Her mouth sought his and Ketter woke.

He was lying on his stomach and his hand was under his body. He was holding himself and he realized that he had come within seconds of the first wet dream since his teenage years. He lay very still, willing the moment to pass, ashamed of himself, fearful that his wife, who lay quietly beside him, might somehow know what had almost happened.

When he arose at last, Ketter slipped out of the bedroom and crept down the hallway to his son's room, careful not to waken anyone. He stood outside Mike's room, listening to the boy's regular breathing.

It was a few minutes before sunrise and the false dawn cast enough light for him to move freely through the house. He walked into the kitchen and ran his hands along the cabinets. He had installed them himself. His fingers caressed the carefully beveled edges of the doors. "This is mine," he thought to himself. He continued through the kitchen and into the living room, touching everything he passed and saying to himself, "This is mine."

It was all his: the house, the furniture, the people sleeping peacefully upstairs. It was what he owned and what he belonged to. It was what he was going to risk, he realized. With a completeness that frightened him, he understood that for once he was going into an adventure in which he stood not to lose his life, but his family, his home, the bedrocks of his existence. And he was going to do it without fully understanding why.

He sat and watched the sunrise, overcome with a deep sadness that gave way slowly to excitement. Karen Maust filled his mind and he could think of nothing else. When he heard his wife moving overhead, he went to his bathroom and shaved with particular care.

Ketter followed her home, pulling his car openly into her driveway and walking quickly to the front door. Karen had entered the house and turned, startled, in the entry foyer, still holding a bag of groceries. It was the noise that surprised her, not the man, and when she realized it was Ketter she grinned.

"It's about time," she said.

He paused for a second, clinging still to some shred of pretense, but as she spoke, he realized there was no need. He stepped toward her and she dropped the grocery bag and came into his arms.

Ketter crushed his mouth against hers and felt her rising on her toes to thrust against him. He kissed her savagely, furiously, as if he could draw satisfaction out of the kiss alone. She responded in kind, clasping her hands on his face and pulling him even harder toward her. His arms went around her back, he grasped her buttocks and pulled her pelvis against him.

They moved into the living room as if buffeted toward the bed by an irresistible current. Ketter was unaware of walking, unaware of even thinking, and yet they proceeded. She was wearing a lightweight summer sweater, which he yanked upward. He mouthed her breasts through the brassiere, then unsnapped it to free them to his touch. With a gasp, she arched her back, pushing her breasts into his lips.

His hands worked frantically, ineptly, at the snaps of her pants. Midway across the living room she halted their bedward drift long enough to unfasten the waist of her pants for him. Never releasing her for a second, Ketter leaned her into the sofa back while tugging the pants over her hips. He fell to his knees and pulled them to her feet. She wore red panties. Ketter pressed his face against them and hugged her to him while she again arched against him and clasped her hands to his head. He insinuated his thumbs under the legs of the panties and ran them upward. She shivered and spread her legs slightly. Slowly he dragged his thumbs across her again, one after the other, and felt her shudder against him.

"God," she muttered. "Yes."

He eased the panties off with one hand, continuing to caress her with the other. When he kissed her between her legs she moaned and spread her legs even farther.

She came to a climax loudly, at first mashing his face against her, then easing him away when the sensation became too much. Ketter looked up and saw the flush spread across her face and chest. Her eyes were closed, her lips parted as she continued to emit a fading series of shuddering moans.

Her breasts thrust forward boldly as she bent back against the sofa. They were a startling pale white against her tan, and the erect nipples were a muted pink. Ketter mouthed one of the nipples and she began to groan again.

He stood and kissed her and she responded ravenously, sucking his lower lip between hers, raking her teeth across his tongue. When he lowered his lips to her breast once more, she shook her head violently back and forth, like a child deprived of its bottle.

Her fingers worked at his belt and shirt, undressing him quickly and expertly. He pressed his fingers into the wetness between her legs and she shuddered violently, as if she had never stopped climaxing, but only paused, waiting for his return.

"Oh God, oh God, oh God," she cried. Her fingers squeezed into his shoulders until he winced with the pain. She released him and seemed to collapse for a moment, her head pressed against his neck and her breath warm on his skin.

He kissed her and this time the aggression was gone from her. She responded, but with a yielding softness that seemed to cradle him. Her chemistry had changed somehow, and her tongue was sweet against his.

They were moving again, though Ketter could not have said how. Her hands were on his genitals, stroking and massaging, feather-light but as if made of fire.

At the door to the bedroom Ketter pulled back and for the first time saw her body in its entirety: the long, long legs, the tiny waist, the breasts that seemed so firm yet felt so soft. She looked at him through slitted eyes and her chest heaved with excitement. For once, the expression of haughty amusement was gone. She was a woman who had come twice and wanted him again. As he watched, she bent and took him in her mouth.

Ketter heard himself gasp with pleasure. She raked her
fingernails slowly up his legs and over his buttocks. His
whole body seemed to be twitching in response to her
tongue and lips.

He gave in to the sensation for a moment, pressing his
hands against her head, then he pulled her to her feet and
lifted her off the ground. He had never had a woman like
this and was not certain what he was doing, but she
responded immediately, wrapping her legs around his
waist and guiding him into her with her hand.

Ketter thrust into her, growling with the effort, holding
her with the strength of his arms and pushing with his
legs.

She took him into her with a fiery compliance and
seemed almost immediately to be working toward another
orgasm. Wrapping her arms around his neck and squeez-
ing with her thighs around his waist, she rocked upon him
as if she would wrench forth her pleasure by sheer vigor.
Ketter staggered, then leaned her against the door frame,
pounding his loins against her.

She came first, screaming aloud this time, then grind-
ing her lips against his, then screaming once more. When
Ketter came, snarling like a beast, she seemed to prolong
her orgasm and shuddered with him.

Suddenly weak, he managed to cross to the bed before
they both collapsed. She cradled herself into the crook of
his arm, her hand upon his stomach, which was wet with
sweat, the hair matted and darkened.

Ketter lay for a moment, not thinking at all, listening
to the sound of their breathing. Gradually the observant
part of his brain returned to ascendancy. He realized what
he had done and how he had done it. Twenty years of
marital fidelity had just been destroyed. The moral superiority with which he had viewed the world had just been
done away with in fifteen minutes of wild, athletic, totally
undisciplined sexual abandon. Whether or not it had been
worth it was beside the point. The simple issue was that
it had happened, that Ketter had known it would happen,

had wanted it to happen, had been unwilling to prevent it from happening. He could not say to himself with honesty that he had been powerless to stop it. With the urgency now past, it seemed that he could have halted it at any time, that he could have shrugged off the obsession like a bad idea.

If it was the first time for him, he was equally certain it was not the first time for Karen. He was glad she made no pretense and no protestation. It simplified matters so. They had done what they had done because they both wanted to do it. If she had any hidden motives, he had no notion of what they might be.

She snuggled against him and his mind returned to his present situation. For the first time he noticed the bedroom, the bed on which he lay, the room in which he found himself. It was intensely feminine, but with a difference that was at first unclear. Only gradually did Ketter come to realize the purpose, and thus the significance, of the items that lay upon the night table and the dresser. Some of them he had seen for the first time in Maust's brochure in Bobby Hauck's office. Some of them he had never seen before in his life.

It was as if Karen read his mind. "Frankie needs help sometimes," she said.

"Uh-huh."

"You wouldn't know much about that yourself, would you?" She ran a finger from his chin to his navel. "You're not a man who needs any help."

"You don't need much either," said Ketter. His voice sounded strange to him. In the days when he had dreamed of making love to her, he had never imagined himself in conversation.

"Not with you. With Frankie, I need all the help I can get."

Ketter propped himself on his elbow and looked at her. He could not imagine any man needing any help other than her presence. She was still the sexiest woman he had ever seen, even though at the moment he felt as if sex was the least important thing in his life.

"Thank you," she said, her lips shifting into the familiar mocking smile again. He was not aware that he had said anything.

On her night table he saw a picture of her and Frank Maust. They had their arms around each other and were smiling broadly at the camera. Frank's eyes became even smaller and more piglike and his double chin more pronounced when he smiled. Why? Ketter wondered. What on earth does she get out of it?

"It's all about sex," he remembered Bobby telling him, but not under these circumstances, surely not with Frank Maust.

For the first time he noticed bruises on her arms and legs, the darkened skin not completely disguised by the suntan. He put a finger to one of the darker areas, traced it gently.

"Frankie?" he asked.

She shrugged.

"Does he need that kind of help, too?"

"Sometimes," she said. "Don't get excited about it."

"Does Frankie get excited by it?"

Karen laughed without humor. "Frankie's a very complex person." She put her hand between Ketter's legs and fondled him. It seemed a startlingly personal gesture to him now that he no longer needed her.

But he soon changed his mind.

Chapter 8

I came to love the thin ribbon of woodland along the banks of the Muddy as much as my father had. It was a dreamland where one could escape the searching sun and the ever-present horizon, a place of surprises and possibilities.

The spirit of adventure seemed to thrive in that tiny forest because concealment was possible there. Dark shadowy places were necessary for some of the soul's yearning, or so it seemed to me. What I did not yet know was that the greatest hiding place of all lay not in the landscape but in the human soul.

Like my father, I had developed a fascination with Indians and the frontier, but unlike him I had turned to the East for my inspiration. I was particularly enthralled with *The Deerslayer* at the time, and it was easy to imagine Natty Bumpo picking his way through the forest, eluding savage warriors while I sat with my back against a tree trunk, the roots of another knuckling out of the ground by my feet and the water of the river gurgling softly only a few yards away.

In time I explored farther and farther along the banks of the Muddy and soon discovered that I was not the only one who sought concealment there. There was an area that one could approach via a dirt road running along the edge of a field. The river took a sharp, whimsical loop there and formed a natural hiding spot for cars where *they could be seen from neither the main road nor the field. It was a popular parking place for teenage lovers and was particularly crowded on Friday and Saturday nights. The lovers could tell if anyone was approaching through the field by the headlights and would have plenty of time to put themselves to rights.*

The only quiet approach, and one never suspected, was by the river itself. It was possible, I discovered, to wade downstream and come at the lovers from their blind side, and more than once I made that silent approach, imagining myself a frontiersman slipping between Indian encampments.

In time, I came there with my lover. I rode my bike to the bridge and hid it in the trees, then walked the half mile through the field to the wooded loop where my lover's car was waiting.

We lay on the bank on a blanket, counting stars and murmuring to each other. I was terrified, virginal, totally inexperienced, and filled with guilt. Like any other fifteen-year-old, I was bursting with sexuality but had only a very confused and conflicted notion of what to do about it. My lover was older and patient and gentle in a way I had never known anyone to be. His fingers seemed to soothe at the same time as they excited.

But when the lights of the approaching car swept across the tree limbs over our heads, he leaped up in fright and sprang to escape. The enormity of our guilt was clearly understood by both of us. There was no need for explanations, no pretense about braving it out. He fled into the night, driving without lights into the field where the corn was now high enough to cover the car. Only when the approaching auto had passed did he dare to regain the road and snap on his headlights. Long after the new car had arrived and the engine had stopped, I could hear my lover bucketing rapidly over the rutted dirt, driving for all he was worth to return to the night and security and anonymity.

I had taken to the river, reverting to my own secret route in the moment of panic and now I was stuck there with the new car facing directly at me. I stood waist deep in water, afraid to move for fear I would be seen. There was no good explanation for my presence, and if my lover had been seen, then my exposure would be disastrous. It was bound to get back to my parents, the scandal would be too ripe to hide. At that moment, I was convinced that I would rather die than be discovered. I stood in the shadow of a limb, but pools of moonlight bathed the river on either side of me. Immobility was my only chance for safety, I told myself.

With a growing sense of amazement, I took in the scene in the newly arrived car. At first glance I thought it was a parent and child. The man's face was in shadow but he appeared to be a contemporary of my father's. The girl sat in moonlight and I recognized her face but didn't know her name. She was several years my senior, a waitress in the hotel dining room where I had attended several of my father's ill-fated campaign functions. He was talking to her urgently, his tone coy and wheedling. I could tell by her expression that she was resisting whatever it was he wanted, but I could not hear her voice over the sound of the water, which was babbling around my legs.

His tone grew more insistent and once he put his hand on the back of her neck, trying to force her down. She was evidently as strong as he was, however, because she pushed his hand away from her and he stopped.

As I watched, both frightened and fascinated, a sense of physical dread overtook me. I realized that while I had been standing immobile, my feet had been slowly sinking into the riverbed. When I tried to pull one free, it would not come up.

Because of the bend in the river's course, a deep concentration of silt had accumulated where I stood. I was sinking into supersaturated mud several feet deep. It was thick enough to give an initial sense of stability, but any-

thing not moving would eventually sink in, as if caught in quicksand.

When the water reached my waist, I became horrifyingly aware that I was drowning by inches. Struggling only accelerated my descent. The mud sucked me downward, engulfing me with the same casual, ineluctable pace of a spider devouring its prey.

In the car, their voices had become heated. They were arguing loudly about something and when I first called out, they did not hear me. Insanely, I tried to keep my voice calm and reasonable, as if the entire situation were a matter of simple misunderstanding that could be solved easily by men of goodwill. No need to show excitement—as if excitement would somehow underline my trespass.

They still did not respond to me and I began to fear that they never would. The man appeared quite upset now, he was gesturing rapidly. The girl had turned her back on him.

I screamed, all pretense gone. The water was at my chest and rising. In the car, the man stopped gesturing abruptly. They both looked directly at me but still they did not move.

"Here!" I cried. "Please, help me!"

The girl started to get out of the car but the man grabbed her arm and stopped her. He spoke urgently to her for a moment in a hushed tone, then got out of the car himself, revealing his face for the first time. It was a face I knew well, but could not believe or explain in this context.

He squatted at the water's edge.

"Well now," he said, his face showing a peculiar smile. "What are you doing there?"

"I can't get out," I said. My tone sounded so casual I couldn't believe it was my own voice. "I'm sinking."

"It's late. Does your dad know where you are?"

"No, sir."

"No, sir, I bet he doesn't."

The water was close to my chest and the current, although not strong, was beginning to affect my balance. I was treading water with my hands to stay upright.

"How do you come to be stuck in the Muddy at this time of night?"

"Just get him out!" the girl called from the car.

"You shut up!" he called back. He turned to me and held an open palm in my direction. I stretched out my arm but could not reach him. The motion made me sink farther.

"You and I understand that it isn't that simple, don't we, son?"

"Yes, sir. Please get me out."

"First of all, I believe I know what you were doing out here. I believe I know whose car that was back there, traveling without lights. I believe I know something about the sexual preferences of that driver, too, don't I?"

"I don't know."

"Don't I know who it was and what he was doing out here, son?"

"I don't know."

He stared at me for a moment with what looked like curiosity, as if I were a newly discovered amphibious creature of the river.

"Looks to me as if the water's coming up on you, son. Tomorrow morning, nobody would ever know you were here."

"She knows." I inclined my head toward the girl in the car. He did not bother to look back at her, as if she didn't exist.

"So what I'm saying, son, is that I know who that was, and what he was doing out here in his car in the night, and that he was doing it with you. That's true, isn't it?"

"Yes," I said, finally. The prolonged exposure to the water had chilled me and I began to shiver.

"All right then. I assume that isn't the kind of thing you'd want your father to know about, is it?"

"No, sir."

"No, sir. You wouldn't. Well, not to worry. Lots of us have things we wouldn't want others to know about. As it happens, a lot of people might misunderstand what I'm doing out here right now. That's why it's important for you to understand that you never saw me."

"Yes, sir."

"Not just so I'll pull you out. But forever. You understand me? I never saw you and you never saw me."

"I understand. I'll never tell anybody."

"Not even your lover man."

The term sounded incredibly filthy the way he said it.

"Nobody," I said.

He watched me for a moment longer. I was trying desperately to keep from crying, but the fear had been growing into panic from the moment I realized there was a chance that he might not help me. My lips were trembling.

"I wonder can I trust you," he said.

It occurred to me for the first time that he might leave me right where I was, that he was actually in doubt. I began to cry openly, my body heaving with sobs.

"I'll never tell!" I said, the words so distorted by the sobs that he didn't understand me.

"Calm down," he said. *"There's still plenty of time for us to come to an understanding."*

The crying shook my body, which accelerated my decline into the mud. I could feel the mud suck over my knees like a hungry mouth. With the greatest effort, I controlled my body, pressing my arms into my sides and willing myself into an attitude of immobility, that seemed, to my tormentor, to pass for calm.

"That's better," he said. *"I don't want you to agree to something in panic that you're not going to stick to later. I want to be absolutely sure you know what's going on here,"* he said.

"I promise never to tell anybody on earth that you were here tonight," I said. I hiccuped once from the tears, but otherwise managed to sound in control.

"And what about me?" he asked. *"What am I going to give you?"*

"You won't tell anybody you saw me," I said.

He paused for what seemed forever. I tried to engage his eye with my most sincere look.

"I'm going to take a gamble on you, son," he said finally. *"Because I believe your father is an honorable man. I don't believe he'd lie, and I believe he taught you to be the same way. And also because I think you know what it would do to him and your mother if they ever found out what you were doing here tonight."*

He got a shovel from the trunk of his car and held it out for me. As I reached for it, he lifted the shovel over my head. For a moment I thought he was going to hit me with it.

"Remember our bargain," he said, then lowered the shovel so I could grab it. The girl came to help and together they hauled me out of the river. I cried and cried, my legs weak and trembling, my arms wrapped around the trunk of a tree. When finally I came to myself, they were gone, vanished into the night.

I never saw the girl again.

In late September, on a Saturday following a victory by the high school football team, a waitress in the hotel dining room was reported missing. Her name was Carol Wittaker. She had moved to Cascade two years ago from Auburn, an even smaller town thirty-five miles to the north. Her purpose had been to get away from her family, which she had done so successfully that she lived in Cascade as if she were an orphan. With few friends and no real ties in the community, her disappearance might not have been noted at all were it not for her job. Several members of the Odd Fellows missed her at their monthly luncheon at the hotel, where they had been accustomed to flirting with her in a harmless, group-protected man-

ner. Neither particularly attractive nor sexy, Carol Wittaker was at least single, and that, for the Odd Fellows,
was stimulant enough.

They mentioned Carol's absence to the manager, who
was more than aware of it because she had left him short-
handed and short-tempered. Bobby Hauck was routinely
present at the Odd Fellows luncheon because he would
devote a column of space on the second page of the *Journal* to their meeting.

By the end of the day, Bobby arrived at Ketter's house,
where he found Ketter, an ax in hand, attacking a stump
in the front yard.

The two friends had not spoken intimately since Bobby's confession of love for Ketter. Despite his efforts,
Ketter felt the admission lying between them like a
chasm, and his own affair with Karen Maust only wid-
ened the gap. He had vowed never to tell anyone about
Karen and already regretted having confessed his attrac-
tion for her to Bobby. Tormented by guilt and self-
disgust, Ketter struggled to rid himself of the lust, but,
like an addict who has sought a cure, he was not certain
that he would not fall from grace again.

The stump, a large one of still-green oak had become
Ketter's source of relief for his physical tensions. He
attacked it with vigor during his free moments, grateful
for its obduracy. Working parttime, it would take him
weeks to hack it out, and he hoped that by that time his
fever of desire would have passed.

It was with relief that Ketter realized that Bobby had
not come to speak of intimacies, but of his concern for
Carol Wittaker.

"I called her house first," Bobby said. "Of course
they'd been calling from the hotel all day. Finally I went
over there. She lives on Howard Street, about a block and
a half from the tracks. Remember where the Stehles used
to live? A couple houses down from that."

"And?"

"The door was open so I went in after I'd knocked. There was a chance she was sick or something, she's alone. I don't know who would take care of her. . . ."

"Are you the visiting nurse now, Bobby?"

"I know the girl, Pete. We've had talks. I was concerned."

"You were concerned pretty early."

Bobby shrugged. "The last girl who was missing from work was Margaret Bletcher. We found her in a corncrib, Pete. Nobody was concerned about Sarah Kiekafer. We found her under the ground."

Ketter felt himself grow warm at the mention of Sarah Kiekafer.

"All right. Go on. What did you find in this girl's house?"

"Nothing. I mean nothing unusual. No clothes missing, suitcases still in the closet. If she left town, she didn't take anything with her."

"Maybe she spent the night with a friend."

"Maybe. And the day, too."

"People do that, Bobby. She's young, right? Maybe she just got fed up with her job and said to hell with it."

"I hope it's that simple. . . . I'd like you to find her, Pete."

Ketter swung the ax and buried it deeply in the stump.

"Harry Killebrew can find her, Bobby."

"It's not something for the police. There's no crime . . . and Harry's no detective."

"Neither am I. I'm an attorney. What's it all about, Bobby? This isn't just random concern."

"Pete . . . I know who she's been seeing. I'm probably the only one who knows. People tell me things. Carol chose to tell me about the man she's been seeing. Not that often, but once in a while. She doesn't like him much, but she does like the attention, she's a lonely woman. And he's a hard man to say no to."

"He's married, I imagine," said Ketter. "That would explain the secrecy."

"She feels uncomfortable about him, Pete. Nothing specific, but she said sometimes he scares her."

"How?"

"It was hard for her to describe. She says it's like sex just isn't enough sometimes. She didn't go into detail, but she sensed a danger."

"Why does she keep going out with him?"

"Why do a lot of us do a lot of things we shouldn't keep doing?" Bobby looked squarely at Ketter, who fidgeted with the ax.

"It's all about sex, isn't that what you told me?" Ketter asked.

"As I said, he's a hard man to say no to. He buys her things. People are foolish."

"Yes," Ketter said, his voice dull. "People are foolish. . . . Who's the man, Bobby?"

"Pete, I can't tell you that. She confided in me because she trusted me."

"You think this guy may have killed her, and you won't tell me his name? That's crazy, Bobby."

"I don't know for a fact that he did anything. Carol may be at a friend's house, just as you said. I can't slander him without any justification."

"I'm not asking you to print his name in the newspaper. Just tell me."

"People trust me. Everyone trusts me. If she turns up at work on Monday and I've betrayed her trust . . . I don't want to do that. To her—or to him—or to myself. Believe me, I have good reasons."

"And if she turns up in a corncrib?"

"Then I'll tell you."

Ketter laughed. "Bobby, I'm not in the people-finding business anymore. Don't take it the wrong way, but I'm not going hunting just because you feel nervous. I quit all that, I came home to get away from it, and I have no intention whatsoever of going back to it."

"What happened, Pete? It was something under that house, wasn't it? Did you finally realize you were human, did you finally get scared?"

"Let's just leave it that I don't hunt people anymore." Ketter pulled the ax from the stump and held it in both hands. "Your waitress will turn up."

"I'm sorry to trouble you."

"No trouble."

Ketter stood with the ax at waist level, ready to resume work.

"How's everything else?" Bobby asked. "Janet?"

"Janet's fine."

"Mike?"

"Mike's fine, too."

Bobby stepped back. His friend's sudden coolness stung him.

"I seem to have touched a nerve," he said.

"Not at all." Ketter swung the ax over his head and into the stump. "It's oak," he said. "It's going to take me a month to hack it out."

"Why bother to remove it at all? It's not in your way."

"It will rot," said Ketter. "Leave it alone and it will rot."

"That's nature's way, isn't it?"

"Nature's, but not mine." He swung again, biting the wood at an angle to the first cut. A small chip flew onto the grass.

"Pete, I'm sorry if I scared you or hurt you or disgusted you, or whatever it is. I can't help what I am. I didn't choose it, but I can't deny it. I'm no different than I've ever been. Please don't let it ruin our friendship."

"Of course not," said Ketter coolly.

"It's hard sometimes to open your heart wide enough to encompass human frailties. I know that, but I thought you could do it, or I wouldn't have told you. I'm sorry if you can't forgive me for it. I would forgive you."

"Nothing to forgive," said Ketter. He wrestled the ax from the wood. "If you don't think Harry Killebrew can do the job, do it yourself. You know more about this community than anyone else. Try a little investigative reporting. What can it hurt?"

Ketter swung the ax again, grunting with the effort, then wiggled the blade back and forth to free it from the stump. Bobby had already turned his back and walked slowly away.

There is only so much crime and violence any community can absorb without reaction. The killings of two women within two months amounted to saturation for Cascade. Anything else would burst the tissue, and both Bobby Hauck and Harry Killebrew did their best to keep the disappearance of Carol Wittaker quiet. It was a futile effort, however, and by the fourth day of her absence rumors swept through the county.

Bobby received a phone call late at night on the fifth day. The voice was muffled, as if to avoid recognition, but Bobby was not surprised. He had already been the object of three such calls, each offering information that was months old and of no real consequence.

"I know about Carol Wittaker," a man's voice murmured. "I will tell you if you'll meet me at your office."

"It's two in the morning," Bobby said. "Can you come in tomorrow?"

"Tonight," the voice insisted. "Tomorrow will be too late."

"All right. Give me a few minutes to get dressed."

"And come alone," the voice said. "If you're not alone, I won't be there."

Bobby reached his office in twenty minutes. It did not occur to him to call the police or anyone else. He had lived a portion of his life in secrecy and had afforded that same secrecy to others. It was his career and his credo.

He parked his car at the curb and walked toward the office door. The streets were deserted at night, as barren of life as the sky. There was no other car in sight and Bobby assumed the caller had parked behind the newspaper building.

Bobby heard one footstep behind him, but before he could turn, a light of incredible brilliance burst in his head. He was not aware of falling, not aware of pain, only of the brilliance. There was another blow that he sensed as an interruption in the light, a flash of color against the sun that was dissolved immediately by the strength of the greater illumination. His ears roared with the sound of the light, and he could not hear his attacker, nor the shovel as it glanced off Bobby's skull and clanged against the sidewalk.

Minutes later, when the police patrol car, prowling the night like a ravenous shark, came upon Bobby's car and moved to investigate, Bobby was still blinded by the light. He was unaware of the blood that trickled from his ear and nose and mouth. He was unaware of the large puddle of blood that had collected under his neck that caused the police officer to assume at first that Bobby was dead. The blood on the cement had come from the scalp wounds, and as such was relatively meaningless. The blood that counted had come from within and had sealed Bobby Hauck within the cage of light in his skull.

On the fourth day the light began to fade and Bobby Hauck could see the dim outlines of the people whose voices he had been hearing for so long. He had long ago sorted them out by their sounds alone, so seeing them would add little to his knowledge. Walt Hogan, the doctor, Bobby's physician. Mary Elise Connors, one of the attending nurses, the one whose voice sounded most soothing. Harry Killebrew, a regular visitor, his deep, unimaginative tones droning on and on. And Ketter. If Ketter had ever not been present, Bobby wasn't aware of it.

He had been by the bedside since Bobby regained consciousness, had sat there day and night, sometimes in silence, sometimes reading aloud, sometimes just chatting pleasantly.

Only Ketter acted as if he understood that Bobby was still there behind the blinding light. The others, and there had been many others, had talked of him, about him, around him, as if he were absent or dead. Only Ketter, from the beginning, had talked past the light. His presence had been like a life preserver in the sea and Bobby had clung to it, following his friend's voice as he struggled back to safety.

But even Ketter had not been able to hear Bobby's screams. Those echoed only in Bobby's brain, imprisoned by the light and by limbs that would not move, lips that would not speak, eyes that would not see.

When the shapes took form, Ketter was seated by the bed, sleeping, his head nodding fretfully on his chest. Bobby looked at the face he had loved so long, the features unburdened of their defenses by the balm of sleep. Bobby whispered his name and Ketter stirred, shifting his weight. Bobby spoke again softly. "I love you," he said. Ketter slept on, unguarded, beautiful. It was a moment of great peace for Bobby and he felt his heart might burst with tenderness.

Ketter woke, startled, and struggled upright in the chair. He looked at Bobby, then around the room, stretching and yawning.

"I love you, Pete," Bobby said again.

Ketter settled back down in the chair, squirming lower until his neck lay against the headrest. He closed his eyes as Bobby called his name louder.

"Pete!" he cried. "Pete! Help me!" with roars so loud they should have made the windows shatter. Ketter slept on peacefully. Bobby willed himself to reach out an arm and touch his friend. Only two feet, such a simple thing, but his arm would not move. A foot then, or an inch, at least an inch. Nothing moved, not an inch, not a twitch.

His arm lay atop the sheet where the nurse had arranged it hours ago after the sponge bath.

The terror swept over Bobby again, complete and engulfing, as his mind kicked and screamed and hurled itself against the walls that imprisoned it. When the panic ran its course, the profound sorrow came, and Bobby wept and wept, but if any real tears ran down his cheeks, he could not feel them.

When morning came, Ketter ritually read the newspapers to Bobby. The *Cascade Journal* first, to reassure him that the paper was still functioning. Then the *Chicago Tribune*, to keep him apprised of the larger world. The papers finished, Ketter took Bobby's hand and leaned his face close.

"You're going to make it, Bobby," he said. "I know you can hear me. You're going to make it. Remember that. Remember it. Hang on to it. I'm telling you you're going to make it out of this thing. Keep at it, just keep trying, just keep coming. We're waiting for you, I'm waiting for you. You can do it, I know it. You can do it."

He squeezed Bobby's hand, hoping for any response, but, as always, there was none. He held the hand for a while longer, not letting his face betray any of the despair he was feeling, and only gradually did he release it and replace it neatly atop the sheet.

Then Ketter spoke of the town, telling Bobby the bits of gossip that didn't make the paper. Only gradually would he come around to Bobby's case. "We still have no clues who did it to you. Killebrew isn't sure it's connected to the killings of those girls because the m.o. is different, but I know it was. You were getting close, weren't you, Bobby? You knew something, or he thought you knew something, or you were about to learn something."

Ketter looked directly at Bobby as he spoke, ignoring the vacant expression, the slack jaw, and trying to penetrate to his friend through his eyes.

"Bobby, I need your help. You know who it was, or at least you know who the man was that Carol Wittaker was seeing. We haven't found her yet. We have to have something to go on. I know you can't move anything yet, but can you blink? Blink for me now if you can control it. Just a blink, Bobby. . . . Can you move your eyes? Can you look to one side? Follow my finger. . . . Well, maybe tomorrow. You'll do it. I know you'll do it."

On the sixth day Ketter interrupted his routine. Instead of chatting about the life of the town, he stood at the foot of the bed and stared at his friend.

"I can't wait any longer, Bobby," said Ketter. "You're going to make it, you're going to be all right, and eventually you're going to be able to tell me who did this to you. But I can't wait, I'm going out to find him myself. I'll still come by, I'll check on you, I'll talk to you, but I'm going to spend most of my time hunting."

Ketter removed a pistol from a holster on the back of his belt and held it flat in his palm for Bobby to see.

"You used to ask me why I quit the Bureau. Everybody thinks something happened under the house where I shot those five terrorists, that I panicked, or got so scared I couldn't live with it anymore, or got disgusted with the necessity, or whatever. That wasn't it. Something happened under the house, all right, but it wasn't getting scared. I'm *always* scared when I have a gun in my hand. Always. I'm very used to that. But something else happened under the house. We were running a diversion, we were shooting flares and flashing lights on one side to get the terrorists looking that way while I closed in. They were panicking, firing like crazy. One of the flares hit the house and started a fire. There was flame and smoke and guns going off. It was like a nightmare and I was frightened, sure, but I kept going and all of a sudden I was face to face with this girl, the one girl in the group. . . ."

Ketter paused, looking inward. He could smell the burning phosphorus of the flare. "Marianne. Marianne Fleming. I knew her inside and out even though we'd never met. I'd lived with the idea of this girl for months, and there she was suddenly, closer to me than I am to you, and she was startled and panicked, with her mouth open, as if she would have screamed if she had the time, and she was trying to get her gun around to shoot me."

Ketter stopped and closed his eyes. He turned his back to Bobby and crossed to the window, looking out for a long time. When he came back, he sat in the chair and took Bobby's hand in his.

"I shot Marianne Fleming, Bobby. I had to, it was the only thing I could do right then, she would surely have killed me." Ketter traced the outline of a blue vein across the pale hand. "I shot her face off, Bobby. I mean, I saw it explode, like a bursting balloon. . . . And then I killed the others. One at a time. I could have taken them alive. I could have disarmed them, given them a chance to surrender. They didn't know I was there with them. I just crept along from one to the next and shot them. They couldn't tell my shots from their own. . . . I did it because I wanted to . . . because I enjoyed it."

Ketter squeezed his eyes shut and pressed Bobby's limp hand against his forehead.

His voice was shaky with anger when next he spoke. "I *liked* it! And I knew I liked it while I was doing it! When I got behind the last of the bastards, my hand was shaking so much I could scarcely point the gun. And Bobby, it was shaking with excitement." Ketter's voice rang with self-loathing.

After a long pause, Ketter rose and stood at the end of the bed once more. He turned the pistol over in his hand several times, then replaced it in its holster.

"That's why I haven't gone hunting since. But I'm going now. I'll see you tomorrow, Bobby." Ketter started out of the room, then stopped, his hand on the door. He returned to the bed and, slowly bending, he kissed Bobby on the cheek.

"You'll make it," he said, and then he was gone.

Chapter 9

With the deaths of two women, the disappearance of a third, and the attack on Bobby Hauck, Cascade was in a panic. Because he was a prominent man and a friend to absolutely everyone in the community, it was the attack on Bobby that made the whole thing appear most real. Some of my friends had been able to adjust to the deaths of the women fairly easily. After all, they fit into a category that obviously excluded those of us who were male and probably even those women who were firmly fixed within a family. The women had been single and promiscuous, in the case of Sarah Kiekafer professionally so, but Margaret Bletcher was thought to have been scarcely less liberal with her sexual attentions. None of us, at least none of my crowd in high school, knew much about Carol Wittaker, which only made it easier for us to lump her with the others. She, too, was single and a working girl, and if her sexual activities were unknown, it was easy enough to assume what they were. By the time she had been missing for a week, the conclusion was drawn that she, too, was dead and buried, even though there wasn't the slightest evidence to suggest it. For the young, there was a certain titillation in assuming the worst. Also, the sexual element—and everyone believed there was a sexual element, again without any evidence—lent a moral air to the killings. No one suggested the women deserved to die for their promiscuity—Cascade was not quite that Old

Testament in its judgments—but on the other hand, there was a strong belief that, had they not been so free and easy with their favors, they would not have been selected for death. It was a comfort of sorts for many.

The attack on Bobby Hauck destroyed that comfort. If a man so harmless and so beloved could be attacked, anyone could be. And anyone could be the attacker. A siege of paranoia affected nearly everyone. The police called for a curfew after dark, but it was hardly necessary since virtually everyone was living behind locked doors from sundown anyway. Rifles and shotguns were plentiful at any time, but now they sprang into sight in the front seats of cars and in living rooms. Several of my friends took to wearing hunting knives on their belts.

Everyone who could not be vouched for personally became a suspect. It was in this context of fear and paranoia that I watched my neighbor, Ellen Hauck, drag herself across her lawn. In the atmosphere of suspicion, she came to look sinister to me. Her dark, old house, unvisited by anyone but herself, took on the tones of evil. It seemed the kind of place wherein anything might happen. I would watch her from my upstairs window, sitting back so as not to be seen, and spy on her for long periods of time.

My father was hunting again, and this time he was strangely public about it. He questioned people on the street, he gave interviews almost daily to the local paper, telling how his investigation was proceeding and when he expected results. He talked to everybody, it seemed, and the rest of us watched, fascinated, as one by one our friends and family were interrogated. Was this man the one? Had this one seen anything, heard anything, suspected anything? In a way it was like a child's game in which the person who is "it" searches a room looking for a hidden thimble and those who hid it look on with increasing excitement as the searcher eliminates one hiding place after another. In this case, however, we knew even less than the hunter.

If my father was working in any official capacity, he never mentioned it. He was simply, by acclamation, the best man for the job. Sometimes he seemed to be in cooperation with the police and other times he appeared to ignore them altogether. He used them when he had a recalcitrant witness, letting Chief Killebrew invoke his official police powers—but recalcitrant subjects were few. Most people seemed eager to cooperate; and waiting for, then "passing," the interrogation became a mark of innocence.

Just what he hoped to discover, what clues, what pieces of the puzzle he aspired to unearth, was not clear to anyone. But then the general process of detective work was unclear at the best of times. And this clearly was of a different order than the theft of a case of beer from the liquor store. There were precedents for that kind of crime. Certain people did that sort of thing and they were constitutionally bad at concealing it. But who killed people? Who came face to face with women and stuck them with a knife then coolly hid their bodies? Who battered Bobby Hauck into unconsciousness in the dark of night?

Because of my father's reputation, it came to be believed that he was operating with a special kind of investigatory divination. He had tracked people across the country, he had pursued them through the years when there were no traces, no trail. He would solve the case, it was believed, because he had special powers.

It was said that there was no avoiding the power of his eyes. It was said that a fifteen-minute session with Pete Ketter was of such intensity that he emerged knowing everything, having scoured the darkest corners of a man's soul with his insight.

Ironically, the thing that had probably defeated him in the election was now what led to his developing myth. It was his personal probity, they said, that rendered him so effective. Living a life of such integrity himself, he could detect sin in another like whiskey on the breath. My father became, within three weeks' time, a sort of Galahad, dis-

*patched on the Lord's work and armed with weapons of
righteousness. The easiest course, it was said, was simply
to tell him everything at once, for it would only hurt the
more when he pulled it from you.*

It was all nonsense.

"*It's a smokescreen*," *I heard him tell my mother late
at night. That evening I had read in the* Cascade *Journal
that he was getting close, that an arrest was imminent,
that the noose was tightening. Now I lay at the top of the
stairway, where sound from the kitchen funneled up as if
from a megaphone and I could hear every word clearly.
I had seen my father's car pull up, his lights the only
ones on the street for more than an hour, and I hurried
to snuggle down for the nightly report he always gave my
mother. I had heard more than news during these nightly
eavesdroppings. The return to hunting had seemed to
draw my parents closer together, as if it put them back
into the familiar and comfortable habits of an earlier
time, and more than once I heard the sounds of passion
and had to scramble quickly into my room before they
came upstairs to their bed. Once they made love in the
kitchen and afterward my mother said, "Something new
has been added. Where did you learn that?" My father
said, "I didn't learn it. I just always wanted to try it."
There was a note of congratulation in both their voices.*

*This night, however, he was speaking of the hunt with
a candor and despair I had never heard before.*

"*I just keep telling lies, throwing more green wood on
the fire, trying to make as much smoke as I can. I'm not
getting anywhere.*"

"*I'm sure you are. You're learning things all the
time,*" *said my mother.*

"*Don't be supportive, Janet. Not tonight. I'm not up
to it.*"

"*I'm only telling you what you know is true. You're
building a skeleton first, isn't that how you put it? First
you need the bones, then you add the flesh until finally
you have the face, isn't that how you always do it?*"

"This case is different."

"You always have a moment when you think you're not getting anywhere," my mother said. *"But you always do."*

"Always before there's been something more to start with. We only investigated certain types of crime at the Bureau, you know that. There wasn't ever much doubt about the motive for tax evasion or racketeering or interstate flight or even terrorism. I was dealing with criminals, damn it. Criminals work in certain ways, they have lives, they have records, they have a past. There are hooks on them, Janet, just by their nature, and all I had to do was latch on to one of those hooks."

"It was never easy, Peter. I've seen you work on a case for months and months. . . ."

"Just to pile up the details, just to make it a neat package for the attorney general's office. Finding the bastards was usually simple enough. You keep asking until someone informs. People don't commit crimes alone—at least not normally. They buy the gun from one person, another drives the car, another cases the joint, another makes the plans, another doctors the documents, another acts as fence. And then the bastard goes home and tells his wife about it, his girlfriend knows, the word leaks out to his drinking buddies, someone in the bar hears about it. Within a week there are so many threads out you'd have to be an idiot not to catch hold of at least one of them. People profit by most crimes, not just the criminal, but lots of people. But nobody profits here. Nobody gains by Bobby's attack except the man who kept him quiet. It's not the kind of thing the guy is going to share with anyone else. He is the only one alive who knows who he is, and unless someone else has seen him, he's going to stay that way."

"Maybe you should ask for help. The state police or the Bureau."

"The state police have already been all over it. They're not miracle workers. There's nothing to go on. The

Bureau can't get into it because it's not their jurisdiction. Murder isn't a federal offense. If the victims were from a minority, maybe we could plead deprivation of civil rights, but they weren't. We can't expect any help and, to be honest, I don't see what good it could do anyway, unless this guy does it again and gets careless.''

"So what will you do?''

"Right now I'm like one of those beaters who goes out on a tiger hunt, banging pots and yelling, trying to scare the tiger out into the open. I hope that if I keep saying I'm getting close, he'll get nervous and do something stupid.''

"You said you thought he attacked Bobby because he was getting close.''

"I'm certain of it.''

"Peter, you are not to use yourself for bait. Do you understand me? You are not to do that!''

I recognized the tone of authority in my mother's voice. It worked well enough with me, but not with my father.

"I can take care of myself a good deal better than Bobby,'' he said calmly.

"You may not do it! Do you hear me? You may not do it!''

"Janet, I'm going to do what I have to.''

My mother's voice was growing hysterical.

"By what right do you jeopardize yourself? You have a family! Don't you care about me? Don't you care about your son? How can you think of exposing yourself to this kind of danger?''

"It's already been done,'' he said. "If he hasn't noticed me by now, he has to be deaf and blind. I've probably questioned him already.''

"But surely you would have known.''

My father laughed. "How?''

"That's your job, you're marvelous at it.''

"Can you tell when I'm lying to you?'' he asked.

"I would like to think so,'' she said.

"You cannot," he said. *"I can't either. With a child, yes, but with an adult? We all become very practiced liars when we need to."*

"What have you ever lied to me about?" she asked.

"That's not the point. The point is, I'm not a wizard, I can't look into people's hearts. I can check their stories, I can listen for inconsistencies, uncertainties, improbabilities. But if a man is a good liar and doesn't blush and stammer every time he lies, if he has sense enough to tell the truth on every point but the important one—I'm not going to find him."

"You make it sound hopeless," she said.

"Without a witness, in this case, yes, it's hopeless. Unless I can make the man nervous. Unless I can goad him into something foolish, he's going to get away with it. With all of it."

"That can't be possible," my mother said.

My father chuckled, low and bitter. *"It's possible. It's probable. The majority of crimes are never solved, I've told you that before."*

"But not the crimes you've investigated," she insisted. *"You solve the ones you're working on."*

"I'm human, Janet. Believe me, I am disgustingly fallible. And right now I'm beaten."

I heard her say, *"Oh, Peter,"* and the scrape of chairs. There was a long silence after that, and I knew that they were in each other's arms, my mother offering him what comfort she could.

I crept back to my room and lay in bed in the dark, thinking about my father. The notion of his fallibility had stunned me. I had disagreed with him many times. Like any other teenager, I had periods when I assumed he knew nothing, understood nothing, had not an inkling of the enlightenment that was my own, and yet underneath all of the adolescent contempt was the rockbottom conviction that he was someone special. My father was, above all else, strength; a sort of granite integrity and competence that could not be eroded by time or circum-

*stance or even my own opinion. He had done all of those
things I had read and heard about. There were the citations and newspaper clippings to prove it. His loss in the
election had not been a failing on his part, but on the
part of the electorate. I had believed the myth with which
the community invested him. Living with him had in no
way diminished my conviction that, in his area of expertise at any rate, my father could do no wrong.*

*But there had been no mistaking the despair in his
voice as it rose from the kitchen. He doubted himself. He
had all but given up on himself. Why then should I cling
so stubbornly to my faith in him?*

*Although I didn't realize it at the time, those painful
moments of disillusionment in my darkened room were the
first steps toward maturity. Once I ceased to view my
father as a divinity, I could begin to see him and appreciate him as a man.*

Since beginning his hunt, Ketter had taken to visiting
Bobby Hauck in the evening before going home. The
agenda of his visits had changed. Instead of reading the
newspaper or chatting about gossip, Ketter now spoke
to Bobby about the day's investigation. In a calm, con-
versational tone, he would recount the interviews and the
histories, the testimony against their neighbors, and
the petty secrets. Many of the confidences that had been
delivered freely to Bobby had been levered out by Ketter's insistent questioning. In his own way, under his own
imperative, he was forming a picture of Cascade that was
as broad and detailed as his friend's. It was not a picture
that Ketter cared for. The facts did not surprise him, but
he had hoped to be able to ignore them in his hometown.

As he related the day's events to Bobby, Ketter
watched Bobby closely, hoping that the mention of a
name would spark some slightest sign of recognition.
Sometime, Ketter was certain, he would mention the name
of Bobby's assailant or the name of Carol Wittaker's

lover—if they were not the same name—and at that moment Ketter prayed that somehow emotion would overpower the physical impossibilities of Bobby's condition.

It did not happen. Ketter was careful never to let his own feelings of despair show through to his friend. He continued to treat him as if he were still there, behind the empty face, listening eagerly.

"Give me another month and I will have talked to every adult and half the teenage boys in this town," he said. "It's like going up into the attic to look for your old high school yearbook. The junk that turns up. All of the stuff you'd forgotten, all the trivia that somebody thought was important enough to squirrel away. I haven't talked to anybody who didn't want to offer some interesting detail about somebody else's life. Do we all spend our days peering from behind curtains? How does everybody know so much about everybody else? Yet nobody knows anything about the man I'm after. I can't think they're covering up or protecting anyone. They seem positively eager to betray anyone. Betsy Rowen told me she thinks her husband sneaked off with one of her kitchen knives. Her *husband*. Turns out he had, he was using it to clean fish. I had Killebrew send it to the state police lab, but I don't expect to find anything on it. Tom Rowen was outraged at the suggestion that he was under suspicion. He said I should start considering the possibility that a woman killed Sarah and Margaret. He wanted me to send all of his wife's knives to the lab, too. Nice couple, the Rowens."

Bobby continued to stare, unmoving. A thin line of spittle trailed from his open mouth. Ketter gently wiped it away.

"Can you roll your eyes, Bobby? . . . If you can roll your eyes, Bobby, I want you to do it for me now. . . . Can you blink? Can you blink today? . . . Well, never mind. Maybe tomorrow. You're going to make it, Bobby. You're going to recover, just keep trying. I know you're trying. We'll all be here waiting for you. There's no rush, it's not a race, just keep coming.''

And when he left the hospital, each day Ketter felt his hope for Bobby erode a little bit more. And each day his hatred of his assailant grew. Somewhere in the town of his birth and childhood, somewhere within the bosom of the town that had nurtured and cradled him there lurked a madman. Or perhaps a man not quite mad enough.

In the third week of his investigation, Ketter returned home to find his neighbor, Ellen Hauck, waiting by the hedge that divided their yards.

"I thought you should know that there was a man outside your house last night," she said. She held herself unsteadily on the crutches she seldom used, preferring to move through the yard by pulling herself with her arms. The muscles in her forearms were as knotted and strong as a laborer's.

"When?"

"About twelve. I couldn't sleep—I never sleep much—and I was just lying there, thinking, when I heard a sound going through these bushes here. Since the curfew, there just aren't many sounds at night. Even the dogs seem to be observing the curfew, Mr. Ketter. How did you arrange that?''

"How did you know it was a man, Miss Hauck?"

She grinned, revealing teeth of startling whiteness. "I looked. Not terribly original, but there you are. It took me a few minutes, but then I could make out his figure. He had crossed through the bushes from my side and was standing just about there, looking at your house. Just staring.''

"Could you see his face?"

"No. I might not have recognized him even if I did. I don't get out much."

"What can you tell me about him?"

"He was about medium height, I'd guess. I can't say anything about his size because all I could see over the outline of the bushes was his head and shoulders. I don't know why, but I got the sense he was a young man, or anyway youngish. Definitely not old, he just didn't move like an old man. I thought at first I should call you up and tell you, but he wasn't actually doing anything, just standing there—it could have been you yourself, for all I could tell, or your boy. Anyway, after a few minutes he went away. It was late, I didn't see any lights on in your house and it didn't seem important enough to wake you for. Then this morning I realized it might mean something to your investigation. . . . Maybe I should have called you right away."

"I'm glad you told me. If it happens again, call me right away, please." He smiled, hoping she could not detect the chill of fear that just passed down his back. "When he left, Miss Hauck, did you hear him drive away? Did you see any headlights?"

She considered for a moment. "No, I didn't. Isn't that odd? Does that mean he lives close enough to walk here?"

"Or that he parked a block away and came through the back alley."

"That does sound ominous," she said.

"I wouldn't worry about it, Miss Hauck. There are always more explanations to a question than we can think of."

She put her hand on his sleeve. "How's Bobby?" she asked.

"They tell me he's about the same," he said. "But I think he's getting better. It's slow, but he's getting better."

"I know you see him every day. I appreciate that, Mr. Ketter. It's difficult for me to get there."

"I'm sure he understands that."

"I'm Bobby's only relation, and I'm not much use to him. I'm very grateful he has you. You're a good man, Mr. Ketter."

"Miss Hauck, if I were really a good man, Bobby would not be in the state he's in right now. Maybe I would be, but not Bobby."

That night, when his wife went to bed, Ketter changed into black pants and a dark turtleneck sweater. Armed with pistol and a flashlight, he splashed himself liberally with insect repellent, then slipped into the night through a cellar window. He took up a post in the garden, lying between the cabbages and the last of the tomato plants, using a flattened plastic garbage bag to protect himself from the damp. If he lay still, the intruder would have to step on him to notice him. By lifting his head a few inches, he could view the entire side yard and the hedge where Ellen Hauck had seen the man.

For four nights he lay there until dawn, feeling the tiny creatures of the night scamper over his inert body as if he were a fallen log. The condensation of the morning's dew soaked his cotton sweater. He arose when the night's darkness began to lift, his body sore and aching despite the isometric exercises he had been doing to keep the muscles alert and supple. In the softness of his own bed, he would sleep at last, but his mind was still straining with the tension of the vigil.

On the fifth day he was exhausted. He took up his post in the garden at ten o'clock and by eleven he was already falling asleep. He rolled onto his back, determined to keep awake by studying the stars, forming random patterns to create his own constellations.

His snore awoke him and he realized immediately that it had also startled the intruder into flight. Ketter heard the running footsteps before his eyes were fully focused. The man had crashed through the hedge and was sprinting through Ellen Hauck's backyard garden, heading for the alley.

Ketter came up running, and made it to the alley twenty yards behind the man. Holding the flashlight with his left hand, Ketter shaped a target on the running man's back.

"Halt or I'll shoot!" he called, automatically voicing the Bureau formula. His right hand pointed the gun, steady but relaxed.

The man was a bad runner, slow and awkward. He stumbled in the rutted alley, his arms splaying out in front of him to break a fall that never came.

Ketter felt his finger tighten on the trigger. The man was an idiot, he had been warned, he had no chance of escape. It would be so simple. Ketter could anticipate the roar of the shot, the slight recoil of the gun like a child struggling against his grip, the acrid, familiar smell of cordite—and the sudden, gratifying collapse of the running man. With a desire that caused him to shudder, Ketter yearned to shoot.

The man tried to vault a fence into another yard and caught his foot on the top pole. He fell heavily onto the fence, then toppled into the yard. With an effort he regained his feet and ran on across the empty yard. He ran straight ahead, not trying in any way to avoid being shot. Ketter held the gun on his retreating back for a full two seconds, long enough to squeeze off a full eight-shot clip.

Finally he clicked his tongue. "Bang, you're dead," he said quietly. The man suddenly fell backward, recoiling from a collision with an unseen clothesline. Ketter was on him before he could stand.

"Please," the man cried, squinting into the light. "I didn't mean any harm." He saw the gun pointing at his face in front of the flashlight. "Oh God, please, please, please," he said. "Please!"

Ketter spread and frisked him on the ground, turning out his pockets onto the grass. There was no weapon. He shone the light in the man's face once more. His name was Robinson and he did upholstery work. Ketter had seen him once with Bobby in the Angler's Club, and when Ketter approached, the man had moved off quickly.

"What were you doing?" Ketter asked.

"Mr. Ketter, honest to God . . ."

Ketter pressed his thumb and forefinger into the man's throat on either side of his Adam's apple, choking him into immediate silence.

"I nearly killed you," Ketter said softly. "I almost put three bullets in your back. Now tell me, and right now without bullshit, what you were doing at my house."

He released the man's throat. Robinson gasped for breath.

"I came to see your son," he said.

There was no doubt that the man was telling the truth. He was too afraid to do otherwise.

"Mike?" Ketter asked, puzzled. "Why did you want to see Mike in the middle of the night?"

"I love him," Robinson said.

The flashlight wavered off Robinson's face and traced an erratic course across the sky.

Chapter 10

I saw my father standing over me as I lay in bed. His face was grim and stony and his eyes looked like angry animals that yearned to pounce on me.

"Get up," he said. It was his slow, restrained tone, the most dangerous. "Get out of bed and come downstairs."

"What's the matter?"

"Now," he said.

I followed him down the stairs. The wooden floors were cool under my feet, but my heart felt as if it had been stunned by an icicle. Before I saw Robbie in the living room, I knew what it was. I had been living with the fear of exposure for weeks, and my guilty conscience seemed to have grown and swollen until it was all there was of me. I was more mortified than anything else at first, but there was relief there, too.

Robbie leaped to his feet as my father and I came into the room. His clothes were rumpled and grass-stained. There was a rip on his shirt, and he held his head at a peculiar angle, as if his neck hurt. He looked as if he had been crying. I vowed then and there not to cry, no matter what happened.

"Sit down," my father said and we both sat at opposite ends of the room. Robbie seemed so unsuitable now, so weak and frightened, such a bad choice for a lover.

"Mr. Robinson here was in our yard a few minutes ago, Michael. When I asked him why, he said he was just looking at your window because he is in love with you. Is that substantially true, Mr. Robinson?"

Robbie nodded quickly.

"I want to be certain," said my father.

"Yes, sir, that's true," Robbie muttered.

My father glanced at me. My expression must have been clear enough so that he felt no need to hear me confirm anything.

"Have you been outside my house at night before?"

"Yes, sir."

"Are you going to make me drag it out of you, Mr. Robinson?"

"No, sir. I've been here like four or five times."

"Just looking?"

"Well . . ."

"What else?" Robbie squirmed in the chair. His eyes never left the floor.

"I went out twice to meet him," I said.

My father turned toward me with exaggerated slowness.

"Why only twice?"

"I didn't want to go the other times," I said. I did not know how to explain the rich stew of emotions that kept me from going every time—fear of discovery, fear of the killer, burgeoning guilt, a growing distaste for the assignations within which I could not separate my disenchantment with Robbie from my emerging ambivalence about the act itself. And over it all, over my entire life, was the event at the river, the shovel poised over my head, the ugliness that forced my silence. The event seemed to have spread over me a film of disgust I could not cleanse. But I could not put any of this into words, so I simply said I did not want to go. It was true enough, for all it left unsaid.

"But you did want to go twice?" my father asked.

I shrugged. "I guess so."

I glanced at Robbie. He looked too frightened to be hurt by my lack of enthusiasm. For my own part, I no longer felt any fear. The worst had happened, I had been discovered. My shame was also my liberation.

My father sat down on the sofa and drummed his fingers on the coffee table. It was built of cherrywood and he had made it himself several years ago.

"Where did you go? At night when you slipped out, where did you go?"

It seemed an irrelevant question.

"To Robbie's garage. He lives about five blocks from here." In the back of the Robinson family station wagon, safely hidden in the darkness of the garage—Robbie had no bedroom to take me to, he lived with his mother. Although a dozen years my senior, he was as much at the mercy of others for shelter and transportation as I. Older, but no more mature than I. Experienced, but no wiser.

"You realize that you can be prosecuted, Mr. Robinson," my father said. He stood in front of Robbie, looking down at him, imprisoning him in the chair with his presence. "Sodomy is still a criminal offense in this state. My son is a minor."

His voice was calm and steady. Only his words were crazy.

"Oh God," Robbie moaned, as if his worst fears had been realized and there were no point in resisting.

"It's not his fault," I said. My throat was so dry it hurt to speak.

"My son is an innocent young man. No, not a young man, a boy, still a boy. You took advantage of him, Robinson. You took a fifteen-year-old boy and wooed him. How old are you?" His voice was heavy with contempt. "How old are you!"

"Twenty-eight," Robbie moaned.

"There are places in this country where you would be horsewhipped for this, Robinson. I knew men who would think seriously about breaking every bone in your body."

"Oh God," said Robbie. *He had buried his face in his hands and his words were muffled. "I didn't mean to do it, Mr. Ketter. I didn't mean to."*

My father paused for a moment. When he spoke, his voice was, if possible, even calmer, more detached than before.

"Are you saying that you weren't responsible for what you did?"

Robbie was shaking his head back and forth, beside himself with fear and humiliation. I knew I should do something to help him, but I could not move from my chair.

"Are you saying it was my son's fault, Mr. Robinson?"

"I didn't mean it," Robbie kept saying incoherently, *"I didn't mean it."*

My father grabbed his chin and jerked his head so his face was pointing toward the ceiling. Like a parent with a naughty child, he held my lover immobile and shamed.

"I'll ask you one more time. Are you blaming my son?"

"No," said Robbie. *"No! Mr. Ketter, I'm so sorry, I'm so sorry!"* His nose was running and tears trailed down his cheeks. *"It was my fault, all my fault!"* Robbie cried. He was out of control now, willing to admit to anything.

"Dad . . ."

"Stay out of this!" He did not turn to look at me.

"It wasn't his fault."

"Stay out, I said. Do you realize what you're confessing to, Robinson?"

I crossed the room and put a hand on my father's arm, trying to free his grip on Robbie's face. Robbie's eyes darted up to me, terrified, like a trapped animal.

"It wasn't just his fault, Dad," I said, tugging at his arm. *"Let him go. He's afraid."*

He yanked his arm free.

"Go to your room," he said, still not looking at me. *"I'll deal with you later."*

"It wasn't his fault," I repeated. Again I touched his arm.

"Go to your room. Now!"

"I wanted it!" I yelled.

"You don't know what you want! You're a child!"

"I wanted it!" I screamed. *"I wanted him! I wanted to do it with him!"* I tugged at his arm again, trying to turn him toward me, trying to get him to pay attention to me.

He whirled and grabbed at me, clamping his hands on my arms. He lifted me and hurled me backward, away from him. His face was in the same grimace I had seen only once before, when he hit his thumb with a hammer.

I toppled backward, flailing my arms for balance. A lamp hit the floor and I became peripherally aware of my mother, standing at the top of the stairs, yelling fearfully.

My father came after me and reached for me again. I raised my hand, making a fist, and threatened him. I heard my mother yelling again, screaming my name.

He was inside my reach before I could strike. Again he grabbed me by the arms, his fingers so strong I thought I could feel them on the bone. He shoved me backward again, into the wall. This time I did swing, hitting him high on the shoulder, my fist glancing into his ear.

It was the last blow I could offer. He pinioned me to the wall, one forearm against my throat, a knee in my stomach, his other fist drawn back. He could have hit me anywhere, I was totally helpless, woefully outmatched. But he hesitated, his eyes glaring at mine. I bit my tongue, concentrating on not crying; it was the only shred of dignity I could cling to. Just not to cry, not to let him know, to keep it inside.

My mother was at his side, screaming his name, pulling his arm off my throat. He could have shrugged her off as easily as he had done me, but he chose not to. He let her pull him off and into the other room.

I could hear them talking in the next room but I was too concerned with myself to pay attention. My chest was heaving with the effort to suppress my sobs. I could not keep my nose from running, or my breath from shuddering, but I did not cry.

Robbie sat slumped in his chair, defeated. He looked as if he would welcome a coup de grace.

Whatever my father said to my mother, it must have at least partially placated her, for he returned to the living room alone, although I could tell she was still in the next room listening. His demeanor had changed, the anger replaced by something that seemed to me intense curiosity.

"All right," he said. "Let's all calm down. Mike, we'll deal with this later. Mr. Robinson, I'd like to ask you a few more questions."

Robbie nodded listlessly.

"Since you seem to be a creature of the night, Mr. Robinson, tell me who you saw on your little visits."

"Sir?"

"On these nights when you were out, did you ever see anyone else on the streets?"

Robbie glanced at me, surprised by the change in my father's tone. He looked as if he believed he might just survive the ordeal after all. My father would never find a more willing witness.

"The town is awfully quiet after dark, Mr. Ketter. Since Bobby Hauck, there's nobody on the streets."

"Nobody at all?"

"A police car once in a while," he said. We looked at each other. Twice we had hidden, flat on our stomachs, terrified that the police had seen us walking together.

"That's all?"

"Yes, sir . . ." Robbie hesitated.

"What is it?"

"How far back do you mean?"

"Tell me what you're thinking. Go as far back as you want."

"Well, this was before Carol Wittaker disappeared, but it's about her. If you're interested."

"I'm interested."

Robbie glanced at me again. I had never told him the details of my experience at the river. I nodded my consent. There was no reason not to tell my father now. He already knew the worst of it. The rest I would leave him to sort out for himself, however much it might pain him, and at that moment I wanted very much to hurt him.

"I was at the Muddy . . ."

"We were at the Muddy," I said.

"And I saw a man in a car with Carol Wittaker. I think it was her. It was dark, but I think it was her."

"You knew about Carol Wittaker, you knew we've been trying to find her. Why didn't you tell me this before?"

Once more he sneaked a glance at me.

"He couldn't tell you because of who she was with," I said.

"Who was it?" he asked.

"Your brother. Uncle Edward." I said it with relish.

The Nyland house seemed to shiver in the night and Ketter's every step brought forth a corresponding creak or groan from the floorboards. He moved through the house with stealthy purpose, guided by a flashlight on the end of which he had fashioned a long cone with paper and tape. The result was a narrow beam that showed him exactly what he wanted to see and little more but was safe from detection from the road by any casual passerby.

He started with the kitchen, searching it with the efficient haste born of long experience. When he moved to the living room, the rocking chair in which Sarah Levy Kiekafer had sat seemed to move with his passage. The air had the musty, wild smell of human abandonment, but it seemed to Ketter that he could still sense the odor of the woman herself.

He had sat with her on the sofa, there. And here she had pressed against him, crying. He remembered with amazement that he had returned her kiss with passion, had put his hand upon her breast. He had not known why he did it then. He still could not understand it, but it was clear that something had snapped inside him on that day. Sarah Kiekafer had freed a side of his nature that he had not known existed, and it had been exerting an increasing force upon him ever since.

As he moved through the darkened house, probing for its secrets with his light, he fought again the battle that had raged within him since that day with Sarah. Whether she had actually done it simply by making the first overt move at him, or whether it had been triggered in some fashion by his return to Cascade, the evidence of the change within him was clear and indisputable. However much he might wish to think of himself as a moral man, as a man who lived his life by effort of will and conscious decision, Ketter had become a creature of passion and impulse.

He continued his search in the bedroom, darting the light into all the places a person might think to hide things. There was a severe limit to most people's ingenuity when it came to concealment. All the ideas that seemed so clever to the uninitiated were routine for a man with training. Lacking the proper equipment and expertise, there simply were not that many "secret" places. Ketter searched them all, hoping more than expecting to find something, anything, that would provide him with the clue he needed. A first step, the initial scent.

The lights of a car swept across the window and Ketter turned to watch it pull into the drive and behind the barn. He moved to the back porch and waited. The headlights died behind the barn and he heard a door close. Ketter turned on his flashlight and shone it toward the ground.

He heard her footsteps, then saw her, walking quickly despite the darkness.

Her face was suddenly in front of him, the features coalescing from fragments of dark. For a moment she looked like a phantom, a witch, with eyes of coal and hair as wild as the wind. She reached out for him and he took her in his arms, lifting her from the ground as he crushed his mouth against hers.

He carried her into the house and laid her on Sarah Kiekafer's bed, which he had covered earlier with a blanket, but she stood up immediately, pressing her body full-length against him. He dropped the flashlight on the bed and it pointed the pencil-thin beam onto the wall.

Karen pulled back from him, standing at arm's length. She put a finger to his chest, holding him in place.

"This one is to savor," she said. He could hear the amusement in her voice, mixed with the smoky sound of lust. "We'll take our time."

Her finger sought his mouth, then caressed his lips. Ketter touched her face, taking his lead from her. He traced the outline of her lips. When she took his finger into her mouth he gasped.

They made love as if they were blind, learning to see with their hands. Her touch was as light as air itself, at times he was not even sure if she was touching him at all, but his skin shivered and thrilled.

When they both were naked, she stepped silently behind him. Her nipples brushed his back, then her hair floated against him. He stood with his arms at his side, allowing himself to feel completely, feeling, just feeling, without doing anything. He felt her breath on his genitals, her hair teasing his crotch. When he reached for her, she was gone, and he heard her laughing gently at his impatience.

He stood, waiting for her touch, his body as tense as that of a man expecting a whip across his back. She made him wait, giving him only her breath, taunting him with expectation until he felt swollen to bursting.

When she touched him at last, he moaned with gratitude.

They made love for a half hour. She tormented him with incomplete pleasures, and he discovered a patience and control he had never exercised before, easing her from joy to joy until finally they sank to the bed together and he entered her. They lay still, locked, for a long time before he began finally to move in a languid way, very slow and very deep.

They finished together, each of them gasping with the release.

Ketter removed the paper cone from the flashlight and propped it so it shone onto Karen's body on the bed. He caressed her nipples, which were still erect, and marveled again at the beauty of her breasts. He lowered his face to her, taking a nipple gently between his teeth. She made a move to touch his head, but this time it was he who stopped her. He kissed the nipple, holding it between his teeth while stroking it with his tongue. When the quality of her breathing changed, he put his hand between her legs. He touched her with a finger and she rose, thrusting her pelvis to meet him.

Within seconds she was bucking against his hand, a desperate note of desire in her throat. She raked his back with her nails and tried to bite his ear, but he pulled away, keeping her pinned on the bed with his weight while he caressed her with his fingertip. She writhed, seeking more contact, but he kept it soft, just out of reach. Finally she collapsed on the bed and left it up to him. He rewarded her by bringing her to another screaming climax.

After a long pause during which he thought she had fallen asleep, Karen spoke to him. The trace of mockery was gone from her tone for one of the few times since he had known her. She sounded grateful and surprised.

"You make love like you mean it," she said.

"I'm learning," he said. "You're quite a teacher."

She rolled away from him with a suddenness that he understood was prompted by hurt and disappointment.

"That's not what I meant," she said, her voice neutral.

He reached out for her and touched her shoulder but she moved even farther away until she was sitting on the side of the bed.

"Karen . . ."

"Never mind."

"I'm sorry. I thought that's the way it was."

"That's the way it was. You have it right," she said, but the defenses had returned to her voice. Once more she was in charge of herself and keeping him off balance.

Ketter was grateful for the darkness that masked his confusion and her disappointment. He was not skilled in the games of emotional badinage. Despite the overwhelming force of his lust, he had never mistaken it for love or even affection. Her lack of sophistication in the circumstances surprised him. He had assumed she was an old hand at the game. It did not immediately occur to Ketter that she might genuinely care for him beyond physical desire.

The flashlight had rolled with her movements on the bed. When she lay down once more it was pointing at her thighs.

"Just think how many of our local citizens have shared this same bed," she said. "I don't suppose you were ever a client of Sarah's?"

"No," he said, feeling instantly guilty.

"I didn't think so," she said. "Far too upright for that."

"No," he murmured, but she ignored him.

"You're probably one of the few who never was. Sarah was pretty good, as I hear it. She made them feel they were special. She put her heart into it. The deserted wife, helpless and alone, seeking comfort from a big, strong man. She probably believed it. Like those girls who have to be told you love them before they'll let you do it. Women are stupid.''

He reached for her again and this time she let him touch her, but her shoulders were rigid as he put his arm around them.

"Karen . . ." He did not know what to say that wouldn't make the situation worse, and he could not give her the comfort she needed because he refused to start lying. It was a curious distinction, he noted ironically, that he would commit adultery with ardor and flair but would not lie.

"Harry Killebrew was one of her regulars, you know. And your buddy Walter Stimpf. Walter has his special needs, but then Sarah was an accommodating girl.''

"How do you know all this?''

"Frankie told me. He likes to talk about sex, any kind of sex.''

"How does Frankie know who Sarah's clients are?''

Karen laughed. "Frankie knows everything that takes place in Cascade. Especially everything about sex. That *is* his specialty, after all.''

"Was he her pimp?''

"My, you do have a low opinion of my husband, don't you? She didn't have a pimp, she didn't need one. A girl needs a pimp for protection, or to feel that she belongs with somebody. Sarah had lots of men to take care of her, that was her angle. As for protection, I imagine Harry Killebrew was all the protection she needed. And Harry took it out in trade.''

"How does Frankie know any of this?''

"Men like Frankie, they talk to him. You can't stand him because you don't approve of what he does, or maybe of what he is, but that doesn't bother most men. He has money and he's not afraid to spend it. He doesn't look down on anyone because of his needs. You don't understand that about him, do you? Men don't like to think someone is judging them all the time. God knows Frankie doesn't judge anyone, and they know that.''

"I'm hardly in a position to judge anyone anymore," Ketter said.

"Because of me? It may be vain of me, my dear, but I don't think most men would think any the worse about you because of me."

"I didn't mean . . ."

"You're just engaging in a little straightforward fucking with another man's wife. I'm talking about men who *need* something. Frankie needs things, and so do a lot of others, and they appreciate someone who understands them. Of course, in Frankie's case, it doesn't hurt to be rich and friendly."

"Don't try to make Frank Maust into some kind of liberal hero. We both know what he is. What I don't understand is why you're with him."

"He made me the best offer," she said evenly.

"I don't believe that. You're an incredibly beautiful woman. I don't know why you're with him, why you're in Cascade, any of it."

"Where should I be? On a movie screen?"

"Yes."

Karen laughed. "People ask me that all the time. There are so many beautiful women. The camera likes some of them, doesn't like others. It doesn't like me."

"I can't believe it."

"It has something to do with the bones. Of course I can't act either, but that's secondary. I tried, believe me I tried. I did everything a girl is supposed to do and then added a few wrinkles of my own. You'd be surprised, but ultimately they want talent. In the meantime a girl has to live. I did a few things for money I'm not very proud of. That's where I met Frankie. He wanted to do a few things too, and was willing to pay for the privilege."

"It doesn't sound like the basis of a marriage."

"What is? I notice you're in bed with me, not your wife. Frankie wanted to show me off: something else he'd bought to go along with the house and pool."

"What do you get out of it?"

"I'm the richest, prettiest woman in town."

"You could have been the prettiest woman anywhere."

"But not the richest."

She laughed at herself and rolled on the bed. The flash-light bounced and pointed toward her thighs. Ketter saw the large bruises at the tops of her legs, livid and fresh.

"Frankie?" he asked, gently touching the skin next to one of the bruises.

"My husband."

"Christ, why do you put up with it?"

"I don't entirely object," she said. Ketter snapped off the flashlight and the room was totally dark. It seemed the safest way.

Ketter heard her before he rang the doorbell, walking through the house alone, singing to herself. Etta wore a housedress, the kind of garment Ketter had not seen in years; he associated it with his mother's generation. He was surprised that they were still manufactured, thought that they had long ago given way to slacks and blue jeans for informal house wear. Etta's was improperly buttoned at the bottom, causing the fabric to pucker and form a discreet opening just above her knee.

Although surprised, Etta ushered him in with an exaggerated graciousness that told him she had already been drinking. He had timed his visit to be certain that she had several drinks in her. "To what do I owe this rare privilege?" she said, smiling.

"I thought we'd have a little talk, Etta."

"A talk? Well, my goodness. That would be nice. I don't get much talk around here. That's a very rare commodity."

"Ed isn't a talker at home?"

She laughed as if he had said something hilarious. "Well now, that's a curious thing about Eddie. He is a great talker, you know, he just loves to talk. However, he is not what you would call a conversationalist. He is more of a public speaker. Edward is not much given to one-to-one conversations. Not that he's at home much in any case.''

"He's a hard worker.''

"Why, yes, he certainly is. A public servant.''

"Still, he must be home in the evenings.''

"Eddie is a busy man. I try not to make too many demands on him. Sometimes he comes home in the evening and sometimes not till late, but I try to be understanding. Will you have a drink, Peter?''

Although born and raised in Cascade, there was something of the southern belle about Etta that allowed her to retain at least a modicum of decorum, however great her need. Ketter had already noted the half-filled glass atop the piano. The air within the house was redolent of fermented fruit, the same brandy she always smelled of.

"That would be nice, Etta. Do you have any brandy?''

"Why, yes, we do. I'll just fetch you some.''

She exited into the kitchen and Ketter took the moment to study the room. It had the gloomy look of a home occupied by a recluse, curtains permanently drawn against prying eyes. He fought an impulse to tear the curtains aside and let the sun in. He tried to imagine his brother's life with this woman. How to square the public solicitude with the private neglect? He remembered seeing Edward tend to her when they drove, as careful and caring as a nurse. Which had come first, her drinking or his neglect? Or had they entered into their pact from the beginning, a symbiotic relationship that did not nurture but somehow sustained. Ketter tried to recall Etta when she had first married his brother, but the girl was now lost behind too many years and too many drinks. At what point had that transformation begun, and when had his brother begun to prey upon the Carol Wittakers? Ketter did not doubt that Carol was not his brother's first venture into infidelity. It pained him to think of Edward in the car with the young woman, importuning with heavy hands for God-knew-what favor.

Etta returned carrying two snifters of brandy.

"I thought I'd join you," she said.

"I'm glad," said Ketter.

"I like a little brandy now and then for my stomach," she said.

Ketter tried to smile. His sense of betrayal was suddenly very strong. He was about to use his brother's wife, to turn her alcoholic weakness to his advantage while prying into her private life with Edward. For a moment he disliked himself intensely. There seemed no justification strong enough to turn on his own family. His world seemed to have crumbled around him, everything he had once valued had turned to dust. The biggest loss, he realized, was his eroding self-respect. Was the quarry big enough for the hunter to lose all he treasured in pursuit?

Etta arranged her dress across her legs as she sat with exaggerated delicacy on the sofa. She noticed the wrongly done buttons, toyed with one, then decided to let it pass rather than draw attention to it.

"Eddie is so proud of you, Pete, you have no idea." Etta prattled on, filling Ketter's silence. "He used to brag about you all the time when you were out there chasing people down. It was such a heartwarming thing to see, two brothers who genuinely liked each other. It's not all that common, as I'm sure you know. I have a sister I haven't spoken to in years."

Ketter willed her into silence, fearful that she would blurt something he didn't want to hear, even without his asking. But still he did not rise, did not excuse himself and leave. However much he despised himself, he knew he would do what he had to do.

"And of course now that you're looking for this terrible man in Cascade, Eddie is just as proud as he ever was. He knows you'll catch him, he just knows it."

"How does he know it, Etta?"

"What?" She looked at him as if just becoming aware of his presence. "He has confidence in you, Peter, that's what I'm trying to say."

Ketter swirled the drink in his glass and watched it spin. "Etta," he said, "it must be very interesting being married to a man like Ed. I mean, an active, virile, masculine man of achievement. It must be very nice."

"Oh, it is, it certainly is."

"Tell me about it," he said, and settled back to listen.

After leaving Etta, Ketter returned to the law offices he shared with his brother. Edward was gone, the rooms dark. Ketter took the firm's checkbook from Edward's desk and began a slow and detailed journey back through time, tracing expenditures, searching through the mundane for the one aberration that would explain everything. He began two weeks after Sarah Kiekafer's death and worked backward.

The lights came on in the outer office and Ketter heard his brother's heavy tread crossing toward the door. Ketter kept the checkbook open in front of him and merely lifted his eyes.

"Did you have a nice chat with Etta?" Edward asked. He lounged in the doorway, leaning against the jamb in a pose elaborately casual.

Ketter looked at his brother as if at a stranger, and realized he didn't really know him at all. They had grown up together, then had grown apart, each following his own particular bent. He tried to remember Edward as a teenager. What had he been like? Was it any indication of what he had become? He couldn't make the connection, the thread had been lost in all the intervening years. They were brothers because they were brothers, an accident of birth, not because they were forever bound by any shared emotion or knowledge. By now, the experience they once had in common was overlaid in each brother's mind by his own interpretation, his own memory, his own emotional and psychological needs. Ketter doubted very much that Edward would even recall the same scenes from childhood. They had spoken of their parents a few times since Ketter's return, and Edward's description of them had always mildly surprised Ketter, who remembered them differently.

He had met Bobby again after the same number of years and knew immediately why they had always been friends. What had formed their relationship in the beginning was still there, the bond still adhered. But what had formed the bond with his brother had been his parents, their family, their shared youth. The family was gone along with the youth. He had no more idea of what life Edward led, what pain he felt, or what joys, than he did of any other man.

He had not known his own son was homosexual. How could he safely say that his brother was not a killer?

"I didn't think you would have been home yet to find out," said Ketter.

"I haven't been."

"Killebrew?"

"Among others. You seem to forget that this is a small town, Pete. You can't get away with much here."

"No. Not much. Not forever."

"Etta doesn't really know much about my business. But I assume you found that out."

"I found out about Carol Wittaker, Ed."

Edward did not speak but his body seemed to slump farther into the doorway.

"What do you think you found out?"

"You tell me."

"Etta doesn't know anything about Carol Wittaker."

"No. It wasn't Etta."

"And how is young Mike? Still seeing his friend?"

"I know about that, too, Ed. He told me."

"You must have some interesting conversations around your house."

"Why, Ed?"

"Why, what?"

"A twenty-year-old girl. No friends, no family. Along comes one of the most powerful men in town. She didn't have much of a chance."

"Chance? She was a lonely girl! What do you mean, chance? I was an opportunity. You don't know anything about it, you don't begin to understand."

"Explain it, then."

Edward barked a laugh. "I'm an attorney, too, remember? I'm not admitting to anything, except that I'm human, damn it! I have needs. I don't apologize for them. You might not understand, but I don't have to apologize for being human."

"What did you do, Ed, offer her candy to get in the backseat?"

"Oh, you smug bastard. You've always been a sanctimonious prick, ever since you were a kid. Always so damned *good*. What the hell do you know about life? There's no trick to being a saint if you've never been tempted. Your kind of purity doesn't mean a thing, Pete, not a goddamned thing. I don't want it and I don't want to hear about it and neither does anybody else. Don't play holier-than-thou with me, just don't do it. Try it on your son. And get away from my desk."

Ketter did not move. Edward stepped toward him angrily, then stopped, aware that there was no way to best his brother physically.

"Why don't you tell me about it?" Ketter said evenly.

"I want you away from my desk, that's my desk."

"Give me your version of how things were with Carol Wittaker. I want to understand."

"Is that your best sympathetic voice? Are you playing at cross-examination now?"

"Where is she, Ed?"

"I don't know. I wish I did."

"Where, Ed?"

Edward sat heavily in the client's chair next to his desk. "You don't know what life with Etta is like. You can't imagine."

"I think I can."

"You can't begin. That kind of loneliness is not something you comprehend with your intellect. You feel it. Like a weight on the heart." He lifted his head. His eyes were moist. "I don't know what your marriage with Janet is like," he continued, "but you talk to her, don't you? You can come home after work and talk to her and assume she understands. You can take her out in public without worrying what she's going to do. You don't get calls from the bar asking you to come take her home. When you walk into your house at night, you don't dread what kind of mess you might find. You don't wake up at three in the morning to discover your wife walking through the house, singing, screaming, cursing."

Edward fell into silence, his chin on his chest.

"I'm sorry, Ed," said Ketter.

"I'm only flesh and blood, Pete. Carol Wittaker was lonely, and so was I."

"I understand."

"Intellectually, you might. I'm telling you, you don't begin to comprehend what it feels like."

"Where is she, Ed?"

"I told you, I don't have any idea. I would have told you if I did, I know you've been looking. . . . Christ, you don't think *I* did something to her, do you? That wasn't me!"

"What happened with Sarah Kiekafer, Ed?"

"Sarah . . . I never had anything to do with her!"

"You were her attorney before you gave her to me. She didn't like the way you had treated her, Ed. What did you do? Were you a customer as well as her attorney? Were you her protector? Was she a good listener, just like Carol Wittaker?"

"You're out of your mind."

"What happened, Ed, did she claim it was your baby? Was she trying to blackmail you? Big politician, you were very vulnerable."

"Is that what the checkbook's about? You're looking for a blackmail payoff? You can't really think I'm the killer! I'm your brother!"

"A lot of murderers have brothers. Mothers and fathers, too."

"You son of a bitch!"

Edward swung at his brother, a futile, off-balance swing. Ketter shoved him back and he tripped over the chair, tumbling to the floor. He did not bother to get up.

"Get out," he said dully. "I'll send your things to your house tomorrow. Better yet, you can have your queer son come pick them up."

Ketter stepped over his brother's body and paused in the doorway. "Because you're my brother, I'm giving you this warning," Ketter said. "No one else knows."

"There's nothing to know!"

"Then there's nothing to fear. But I'm going to keep looking, Ed, and now I know where to look. I'm not going to stop until I've got you tied up like a shoelace. I'll do whatever I have to. You are my brother. Protect yourself."

Ketter walked through the outer office. When he reached the door, he glanced back to see Edward getting to his knees.

"Protect yourself," he said again.

"You do the same," said Edward. "You're not invulnerable."

"No, but I'm . . ." Ketter stopped. He was going to say "innocent," but he realized how untrue that was.

He left the office and walked home in the night. A police car passed him once and slowed, but when he moved toward it, the car sped away. Ketter could make out the massive form of Harry Killebrew behind the wheel.

Chapter 11

My father had said we would talk later, but we did not. I waited like a man on death row awaiting the approach of the chaplain who will lead him to the executioner. The waiting came to seem worse than the sentence, an inhumane forestalling of the inevitable. I wanted to be put out of my misery, although I did not know what that meant in terms of my father. I did not want forgiveness—I did not feel what I had done was wrong. It was what I was, how I felt, and there was no need to apologize. What I wanted, I think, was to be absolved for having disappointed him. To be complete, I know now, that absolution could only come from myself. But I did not understand that then, and all I looked for at the time was some sign, some flicker of recognition from him to the effect that he did not hate me for spoiling the meaning of his life. I did not receive it. I did not receive anything. He turned his back on me as totally and completely as if I did not exist. I think, for a time, that was exactly what happened. He simply put me out of his mind until he had the time to deal with me. He was deeply immersed in the hunt for the killer—more so than ever—and was seldom home, and even when he was, he was scarcely with us in mind or spirit.

I suffered from his absence, but I was not the only one. My mother also felt his withdrawal very keenly and had been feeling it over a period of a few weeks. Their late-night talks, on which I had so avidly eavesdropped, had ceased. I heard no midnight murmurs from the kitchen or their bedroom.

She became uncharacteristically edgy and excitable, almost skittish, like an animal that sniffs an approaching danger. She was deeply concerned about my father, although she tried hard to keep it from me.

"I've never seen him quite so obsessed with a case before," she said in explanation of his withdrawal. "It's not just work this time."

"He's changed," I said. "He's different than he used to be."

She moved away from me as if she wanted to avoid the subject.

"He's busy," she said. "He'll come back to us once this is over." But she didn't convince either of us. We were both losing him. I at least knew why. But what my mother had done to alienate him, neither of us knew.

And yet, oddly, it was a good period for my mother and me.

She had taken the discovery of my sexuality extremely well. It had been her reaction I had feared most in the nights when I lay awake, dreading what would happen when they knew. I had predicted hysteria and self-recrimination from my mother, followed by questions, endless questions eliciting answers that would settle nothing. But I had been wrong. She seemed sad for a day, but then she rebounded with an outpouring of interest and affection. It was as if by looking at me in a new way she had created a new person, and now she was eager to get to know this welcome stranger.

We talked more, and more openly, than at any time since I had reached puberty. Where before she had spoken to me like a parent, she now began to speak to me as an equal, and it unleashed a torrent of talk that she had been storing up since moving to Cascade. She had always felt like an outsider in my father's town and had conducted herself with a measured reserve among the *other women. That fine judgmental eye she had inherited from her mother had toted up the local ladies and found them all wanting in some particular of style or taste or intellect.*

My father had never been a suitable partner in her snobbery—he did not like gossip at home, it too closely resembled the investigative rumors with which he dealt at work—and there was an aura of dignity about him that made one feel petty when trafficking in the lower human pleasures. Worse, he did not share my mother's assumption of superiority over everyone in town. He did not think that being a citizen of Cascade was in itself a sign of failure.

But now, at long last, my mother found a soul mate in me. Since it was my most ardent desire to leave Cascade as soon as possible, I was more than willing to join her in cattiness about the inhabitants. I think she had always feared I would turn into a copy of my father, imbued with that forbidding male rectitude. I was not, and she was delighted, and we had a good time together.

It was only when my father was home that our shared enjoyment was palled. She was torn, then, between the two of us and our conflicting needs. He won, ultimately, and she spent her time with him, trying, vainly, to breach his wall of silent intensity, and to return to the inner reaches of his life that had recently been sealed off from her. What they talked about in private I can only imagine, but I think she was urging him to forgive me, or at least to deal with me, to treat me as if I were still alive, still in his house, still his son. He either didn't hear or didn't heed, because he continued to act as if I weren't present.

When he would leave the house, she would watch him go with sorrowful, fearful eyes, as if he were going off to be swallowed by the world, never to return. I did not know exactly what she was afraid of, and I suspect she did not either, except that it was vague but real, and it

fell under the same name as what I was feeling. We were
both afraid of losing him.

Ketter found Bletcher in the feedlot, shoveling corn to his
hogs from the flatbed of a truck. The animals jostled each
other noisily, squalling with excitement and protest. Ketter had never cared for hogs. Belligerent and independent, they seemed too intelligent for their destiny and
gave Ketter a sense of discomfort when he thought about
them.

He waited impatiently for the commotion to subside,
watching Bletcher work, concentrating on the heavy muscles of the man's forearms rather than the rooting animals. Bletcher took his time, doling out the last scoopful,
then sweeping the truck bed with the flat end of the
shovel.

They walked toward the farmhouse, Ketter stepping
delicately around the puddles and piles while Bletcher
strode straight ahead with a farmer's indifference.

"We talked before," Bletcher said.

"I thought we ought to talk again," said Ketter.

"Does that mean I'm a suspect?"

"No, it means I wasn't asking the right questions
before," Ketter said.

"I meant to tell you last time but it slipped my mind
once we got to talking—I'm sorry about the election."

"Ah." Ketter had not yet learned an appropriate
response. People offered condolences as if he were in
bereavement.

"I say that because I voted for you."

Ketter was surprised. "I wouldn't have thought so."

"I gave you a hard time at your speech because I
thought you ought to know about Maust's operation. I
could see that you didn't, then I heard you made it your
business to find out."

"That's right. It's Maust's operation I wanted to talk
to you about today," said Ketter. "Maust told me he fired

Margaret because she wasn't honest. What can you tell me about that?''

They settled on the farmhouse porch. Bletcher collapsed into a worn rocker as if exhausted.

"Margaret was honest. If you're talking about money and that sort of thing. I've been learning a lot about my girl since she died, Mr. Ketter. A lot of it, a whole lot of it, I'm not glad to hear about. But she wasn't a thief. That ain't why he fired her.''

"Why did he fire her?''

Bletcher took a very long time to fill and light a pipe.

"Did she ever tell you why she was fired?''

Bletcher spoke from behind a cloud of smoke.

"It was personalities, she said. She didn't get along with Maust.''

"Did you believe it?''

"As far as it goes.''

"What else is there to it?'' Ketter asked. He felt Bletcher's resistance even though nothing had outwardly changed. "What kind of relationship did they have, Mr. Bletcher? Did it go beyond employer and employee?''

"You're talking about my daughter, Ketter.''

"I'm trying to find her killer.''

"There's some things won't do you any good to know. I'd never swear to them in court.''

Ketter shifted his position on the porch railing. "Mr. Bletcher, this case is never going to be solved in court.''

Bletcher looked at him, puzzled. The pipe smoldered in his hand.

"What does that mean?''

"It means that some things can be proven in a court of law and some can't. Whatever you tell me about your daughter and Frank Maust is only hearsay. His attorney would have it thrown out. But I'm not going to throw it out. And I'm not going to repeat it. It's for my information only. Did Margaret have an affair with Maust? Did she sleep with him?''

"You're talking about my baby girl, goddamn it!" Bletcher leaped to his feet and for a second Ketter thought he might hurl him from the porch. Then he turned his back to Ketter and after a moment his shoulders sagged.

He walked into the farmhouse and Ketter followed. After rummaging for a moment in the back of a desk drawer, Bletcher withdrew a tattered manila envelope. He turned it upside down over the desk, as if discarding garbage. Half a dozen photographs fell out.

"She always told me she worked in his office. I believed that, she was a good typist, and at first I didn't really understand what exactly goes on there at that place. Most of the people around here don't know, you'd be surprised. The people who work there don't know half the time. They're just stamping things and addressing packages and I don't know what all. It's not a business anyone is talking about much."

Ketter spread the photos on the desk. They were pictures of a young girl in a Nazi uniform, a whip in hand. In one shot, a naked woman was chained to a table, her face averted from the camera. The Nazi girl's whip was dangling over the naked woman's buttocks, on which red welts showed the marks of violation. In another shot the Nazi girl stood behind her victim, who was blindfolded, and threatened her breasts with a burning cigarette. The Nazi was leering sadistically at the camera, an effort at acting that could not overcome the basic innocence of the girl's face. She looked like a child playing in her mother's clothes, going through the motions without any real understanding of the significance.

Ketter remembered one of the photos from this series in the brochure that Bobby had shown him.

"I found these in Margaret's room after she was killed," said Bletcher. "They were taped on the bottom of one of the drawers."

Another of the photos showed the naked woman, still blindfolded, on all fours in front of the Nazi, who was whipping her on the back. There were welts on her back, which had not been in the previous pictures. Either a makeup man had been conscientious, Ketter thought, or the welts were authentic. They looked real enough to him. A man stood behind the victim's upturned buttocks. He held a huge dildo in his hands. Ketter was about to discard the photo when he noticed an incongruous detail and looked again. The victim was smiling.

"It must have come to something that Margaret wouldn't stand for," Bletcher said. "There's only so far you can bully or push anybody, I don't care how good the job or how good the pay. When she had enough, she must have told him so. They fought and he fired her. I'm just putting it together afterward, you understand. If I'd known any of this at the time, I would have burned Maust's place to the ground and him with it."

Ketter looked up from the photos. Bletcher had his pipe clenched between his teeth, staring at the wall.

"Mr. Bletcher, is this your daughter?"

Bletcher glanced at Ketter's finger, which lay on the likeness of the young Nazi.

"No," said Bletcher. "The other one."

Ketter looked again at the blindfolded victim, naked on all fours, whip on her back, dildo about to violate her. He couldn't imagine what it was Maust might have wanted that Margaret Bletcher thought was too much.

"Why didn't you tell me about these before?" Ketter asked.

"Would you?" Bletcher replied. He drew loudly, savagely, on the pipe, which had gone out. He spent a long time relighting it, concentrating very hard on the simple act.

The state police polygraph technician was a heavy, tired man who had witnessed too many years of sweat and lies and frantic, nervous self-justifications to be very surprised at anything. He had examined men and women and children, many innocent, many not, not a few who were too excited or intimidated or manipulative—or guilty—to provide a meaningful reading on his machine. But this was the first time he had ever monitored the responses of someone who couldn't even blink.

Skoura, the technician, sat at the end of the hospital bed, his machine in front of him. Wires snaked from the machine, connected to sensors gauging Bobby Hauck's blood pressure, breathing, pulse, and the electronic potential of his skin. Skoura could measure them all on his metered graphs. He had never contended he could learn the truth of a matter—only that he could detect excitement.

"I don't understand," said Dr. Hogan. He had carefully observed the application of Skoura's sensors. They did not concern him, they were only variations of appliances the doctor himself had used many times. What concerned Dr. Hogan was the test itself.

"If he can't answer, how can he lie?" he continued.

"I don't want to find out if he's lying, Walt," said Ketter. "I want to see what he reacts to. The lie detector measures autonomic responses a person can't control. If something causes him to have an unusual reaction, the machine will chart it. Whether or not it's a lie is a matter of interpretation, but the reaction itself is a matter of fact. It shows up on the graphs. If his breathing changes or if his pulse changes in response to a question, then we can assume that the question has in some way stimulated him. Right, Skoura?"

Skoura shrugged. "If his signs change, they'll register on the graphs. That's all I can say. If you're asking me will it work, I have no idea. I've never done it. And I certainly won't be responsible for making any sense out of it. But basically, Doctor, my sensors will show the same things yours do, the only difference is it's on a graph in permanent record."

"I think it's fairly crazy," said Hogan, "but I don't see what it can hurt."

"It's worth the try," said Ketter. "We ready, Skoura?"

Skoura flicked a switch and the graph paper began to feed slowly through his machine. Four styluses scratched a record of Bobby's signs.

"We're running," said Skoura. "Just talk to him for a minute and give me a base reading."

"Bobby, you understand what we're doing," said Ketter. "I'm going to talk to you and ask you some questions. I know you can't answer directly yet, but if I ask the right questions, your body is going to react and that will give me an answer. I don't want you to try to do anything to make a difference. Just relax and let your heart do it. If it's the right question, your heart will react and your skin will react, without your actually doing anything." He turned to Skoura and saw the graphs moving in steady, rhythmic patterns. "Okay. Let's get on with it. Bobby, I'm going to ask you a few questions, then this will be over. I want to talk about Carol Wittaker."

Skoura bent over the polygraph.

"You told me she was seeing a man, Bobby. You thought that man was capable of hurting her. Was that man Harry Killebrew?" Ketter paused, waiting for Bobby's reaction, if any, to subside. "Was the man my brother, Edward?" He paused again, glancing at Skoura, who watched the graphs intently, as if he expected them to speak to him directly.

"Bobby, was the man Carol Wittaker was seeing Frank Maust?" Ketter paused, listening for Skoura's voice. He realized that he was involuntarily holding his breath. "Was the man Walter Stimpf?" Ketter stopped, then squeezed Bobby's hand and carefully placed it atop the sheet, in their normal ritual. "Let's get this stuff off him," he said to Skoura.

As Skoura wheeled his machine out of the hospital room, Ketter bent over his friend. "You're going to be okay," he said.

"Keep fighting, you're going to make it. We're all waiting for you, just keep trying."

Skoura was waiting in the hospital administrator's office, the graph sheet stretched over a desk. Skoura made notations and large ellipses around the spiked lines.

Ketter closed the door behind him. The two men were alone.

"Well?" said Ketter.

Skoura looked up from the graph.

"What did you expect?"

"I don't know," said Ketter. "It seemed possible."

"Yeah, well. Possible, maybe."

"Did you get anything?"

"Of course I got something, I got his pulse, I got his breath rate, I got all the stuff any doctor could give you."

"But no reaction?"

Skoura turned the graph so Ketter could see it.

"No reaction."

"No reaction to anything?"

"It's possible you didn't ask the right questions, I suppose. But again, only possible. I'm afraid you got to figure the man isn't responding because he can't."

Ketter turned and faced the wall until he was quite certain his distress would not show.

"You haven't told anyone else what you have here?" he asked.

"No."

"Skoura, here's what I want you to do. Don't tell anyone about your results. I mean no one. Not your wife, not your dog, nobody. I want you to go out to your car right now and leave Cascade. Don't stop, don't talk to anybody, don't even get gas. Keep driving until you get back to the capital. If anyone tries to contact you and asks about your results, tell them they were confidential and refer them to me. Then let me know about it right away. All right?"

"If that's what you want."

"It's important. Very important."

"You got it, Mr. Ketter. They told me to cooperate with you and that's what I'm going to do."

Ketter folded the graph paper and put it in his pocket, then escorted Skoura to his car in the hospital parking lot.

"Don't talk to anyone."

"Who am I going to talk to? I'm leaving right now."

"If the police stop you, just clam up and say you gave the report to me."

"The police? Why are the police going to stop me? What am I getting into?"

"Just drive, Skoura."

Skoura drove out of Cascade, watching his rearview mirror until he was twenty miles out of town. Only then did he relax and convince himself that Ketter was crazy.

At the hospital, Ketter returned to Bobby's room. He held the graph in front of Bobby, then waited until the nurse entered the room.

"It worked, Bobby," he said. "We're going to get the bastard now."

Ten minutes later he passed Dr. Hogan in the hall. When Hogan asked about the results of the test, Ketter said, "I can't comment on that right now." Then he let his smile tell the lie for him.

Walter Stimpf had the vague, distracted air about him of a man living in a house with many children. He seemed unable to fix his attention on any one thing very long because he was always listening for the activity in the next room to need his presence. He carried the attitude to work with him, and it made him seem busy and preoccupied to some people. To Ketter it made him seem shifty. It was almost impossible to hold his eyes in a gaze for more than a second or two before they darted off, looking for something safer. He reminded Ketter of a rodent looking for a hole.

"What I have, Walter, is evidence that won't suit a prosecuting attorney. It wouldn't satisfy a judge or jury."

"I see," said Stimpf. He took a tissue from his desk and dabbed at one nostril.

"It would satisfy an agent that he had the right man, though. It satisfies me."

"You mean you have him? You know who it is?"

"I know who I suspect," said Ketter. "There aren't really that many possibilities if you consider motive. The first killing was Sarah Kiekafer. She was expecting money, sizable money. I think she was blackmailing someone, probably by claiming he was the father of the dead baby. It had to be someone in this community who was wealthy enough to pay her blackmail, and important enough to fear her disclosure. Most men would be embarrassed if it became known they frequented the local prostitute, but not enough to kill for it. It had to be somebody who had a lot to lose, a position, a reputation, an election."

Stimpf laughed uneasily. "You're not . . . uh . . ."

"I'm not what, Walter?"

"Never mind."

"I know who her clients were, Walter. I know who she looked to for protection, I know who 'befriended' her."

"You can't be certain you know them all, surely."

"I know them, Walter. All of them."

Stimpf stood and walked to the window, turning his back on Ketter.

"I think he killed her to keep her quiet, to keep her from ruining his life."

Ketter turned the gold-framed photograph on the desk so he could see it. Stimpf's eight children were clustered around their father and their mousy mother in the proto-type for the election flyer that Ketter had held in such contempt.

"Fine-looking family," said Ketter when Stimpf turned from the window.

"Thank you. And why did he kill the others?"

"One other. Margaret Bletcher."

"And Carol Wittaker," said Stimpf.

"Carol Wittaker is missing, unless you know something I don't know, Walter."

"No."

"No, of course not."

Stimpf returned to his desk and turned the photograph so it faced his chair.

"So why did he kill the Bletcher girl?" he asked.

"I think he killed Sarah to protect himself," Ketter said, "but it had an unexpected bonus. I think he found that he liked it. I think it gave him a thrill that he couldn't get at home."

"You think it's all about sex, then?" said Stimpf.

Ketter paused, remembering the phrase from Bobby's lips.

"Yes," he said, "I think it's all about sex. And I think Bobby knew it and knew who the killer was, or suspected it. I wouldn't help him, you see. I wouldn't get involved. Didn't want to dirty my hands. So he tried to find out a bit more on his own. That's why he was attacked."

"Did Bobby tell you who he thought it was?"

"No, he didn't. It was someone whose reputation or position was too important to be jeopardized by loose talk. He wanted to be sure. He respected the man, or feared him. Again, that limits the suspects to the same few, don't you think, Walter? There aren't many people in this community that Bobby would need fear. Except someone in a position of power."

"This is all very thin supposition, of course."

"Of course. I told you it wouldn't be enough for you to bring an indictment. But there is more. I found out the name from Bobby."

"You said he didn't tell you."

"Not directly. I used a polygraph and asked Bobby those few names and I got a very strong reaction on one of them."

"A polygraph is not admissible in court."

"I know that. Even less so when used on a man who cannot speak. But it convinced me, Walter."

"Who is it?"

Ketter paused, trying to fix Stimpf with his gaze. It was impossible, the man wriggled away almost immediately, taking another tissue and dabbing his nose.

"I can't tell you, Walter, not until we can arrest him. It's for my own safety. When he learned that Bobby knew his identity, he tried to kill him."

"You can tell me, for heaven's sake. I'm the county attorney."

"It's my life, Walter. I have a family, too, you know."

"We'll provide you with protection if you think you need it."

Ketter laughed. "Who? Harry Killebrew? I'd rather take care of myself."

"You aren't suggesting that Harry . . . not Harry. I've known Harry all my life."

"I'm not suggesting anything or anyone. I know what I know, and now it's a matter of putting together the final piece of evidence."

Stimpf was on his feet again, moving back to the window.

"How are you going to do that?" he asked.

"I shouldn't tell you."

"I think you know you can trust me, Pete."

"Do I, Walter?"

"Of course you can."

Ketter smiled ironically. "In the Bureau, it was occasionally necessary to be a bit creative when it came to evidence. Not often, but once in a while an agent had to supply the missing evidence to make a case concrete."

"Are you talking about planting evidence?"

"I'm talking about a man who has killed two women, maybe more. What is the greater evil, Walter? What is in the best interest of the people?"

"I can't listen to this. You can't tell me this. I'm the county attorney."

"Once that bit of evidence is there, all the rest will fall into place. We can bring the state people back in, we'll do all the blood tests and fiber tests and put the son of a bitch under the microscope. All we need is the first bit of evidence for the police to find. If he's not guilty, then that will come out, too."

"Jesus Christ, Pete. You can't do that."

"No, Walter, *you* can't do that. You're the county attorney. I'm a private citizen with only my own conscience to answer to. After all, how will anyone know if the evidence is planted or real? Believe me, I'll only put it where it will do the most good."

"I won't listen to any more of this."

"In that case, forget all about it. I'm sorry to have taken up your time."

Ketter walked to the door and paused, his hand on the knob, waiting for Stimpf to look directly at him.

"This must remain between us, Walter."

"Of course! Christ! What did you think?"

"I'm counting on you, Walter."

Stimpf nodded ardently, eager to get Ketter out of his office.

On the way to his car, Ketter allowed himself a tiny smile of congratulation. Go, Walter, tell your friends, he thought. Let the son of a bitch know I'm coming. It was like blowing smoke down a hole in the hope of smoking something out. Ketter did not know if anything was in the hole, but he had no option. He was going to blow smoke in every hole he could find. Something had to appear eventually, he hoped. The danger, of course, was that he didn't know what might emerge, or where, or when. With so many holes, it could very easily come up behind him, when his back was turned and vulnerable.

Their lovemaking had become an exercise in technique, each of them directing the other through a series of changes, like sexual acrobats showing off. No session was without at least two different positions, each more exotic than the one before. But not more satisfying. The great heat of passion that had propelled them through their first meetings had cooled to a kind of dogged determination. They had sex, Ketter thought, because they had decided to have sex. That is what lovers do, so that is what they did. The problem, he realized, is that they were not lovers, they were sexual partners. And the fault, of course, was primarily his own. He had brought nothing to their union except lust, and when she had reached out for more, making a claim on his affection and intimacy, he had pulled away. His affection and intimacy were spoken for, long since promised and, with moderate success, delivered to his wife.

He lay on Sarah Kiekafer's bed in the darkness, staring at the ceiling, exhausted, but not at ease. Karen lay with her head on his arm. She stroked him with her hair, splaying it across his chest. She aroused him as much as ever, he realized. He wanted her with as much ardor as he ever had—but the need was no longer sufficient to justify the act.

"I won't be seeing you again," he said finally.

"I know," she said.

"You don't mind?" He could feel her shrug.

"Do I have a choice?"

"Not really."

"Then I don't mind," she said. "What could I do to keep you? I can offer a man my face and my body and a certain expertise. You've had those and they weren't enough to keep you. What should I do, cry and beg?"

"You have more to offer than that," he said.

"Save the gallantry. I knew we'd get to this point sooner or later. It's just a little sooner than I had hoped."

"I love my wife," he said.

"Or you want to think you do, anyway. In your case it's the idea of loyalty that you're loyal to, but it comes to the same thing in the end."

Ketter was silent for a moment. He tried to see her in the blackness of the room.

"I'm beginning to think everyone knows me better than I know myself," he said.

"Oh, you're easy to read," she said. "Tons of morality laid on top of very human feelings. You're fine until one of those feelings acts up, then all that integrity cracks. Now you're putting it back into place."

"It counts," Ketter said. "Morality counts. It has to."

"Sure it counts," she said. "But it cracks, too. That's your problem, you don't realize that, and you can't stop hating yourself because your humanity shows through. You're a lot more human than you want to admit."

"I'm learning," said Ketter.

"You're a good man, Ketter. That's what attracted me to you in the first place. Everybody wants a piece of goodness. But not too much."

"You have to make the effort to live the way you feel is right," said Ketter. "It's just chaos if you don't try."

"So, keep trying," she said. "Just don't forget to forgive yourself if you fail."

"Do you forgive me?"

She laughed. "I forgive everybody," she said. "That's my problem."

He walked with her to her car behind the Kiekafer barn and embraced her, knowing it was for the last time. Her lips were warm and soft and her breath sweet, as it always was after they made love. Even as he released her he knew he would miss her. Despite what she said, he loved more than her body, but she was not part of how he wanted to live, how he needed to live to be proud of himself.

He watched her drive off, following her red taillights until they vanished from sight. He wondered for a moment what it had all been for.

The headlights hit him like a physical force, snapping on in the darkness and pinning him against the barn. He waited, feeling trapped and guilty.

"Hello there, Mr. Ketter," said a deep voice. "Nothing like a little late-night fun with the wife, is there? Not your wife, of course, but still fun, I'd bet."

"What do you want, Harry?"

"I wouldn't mind some of what you just had, for starters," said Killebrew. He got out of the squad car. When Ketter moved out of the headlights, Killebrew followed him with the spotlight. "How do I go about getting some? Ask Frankie, or what?"

Ketter walked toward the squad car. "Get that light out of my eyes, Harry."

"I understand you've been bothering Walter Stimpf with your opinions. Walter has enough trouble with facts, Pete, don't confuse him with opinions. For instance, he tells me you think I might be the man who murdered Sarah."

"Get the light out of my eyes or I'll stuff it down your throat," said Ketter.

Killebrew moved so that Ketter could see his arm in front of the spotlight. He held his police automatic in his hand.

"I'm a cop, Pete. Nobody stuffs anything down my throat that I don't want to swallow. Including you. Especially you."

Ketter glanced for a place to hide, the quickest refuge he could reach.

"I know about your relationship with Sarah Kiekafer, Harry."

"Fine. And I know about your 'relationship' with Karen Maust. *Mrs.* Maust, that is. I don't know if your wife knows, though. Does she know, Pete? Have you told her yet?"

"What do you want, Harry?"

"I don't want anything, Pete. I'm just out doing my job. Thought you'd like to know that I'm here, keeping my eye on things, covering your back, so to speak. I wouldn't want you to feel vulnerable, considering the good work you're doing and all. Just remember, when times get tough, old Harry is right behind you.''

Killebrew got into the car, trod on the gas, and slewed it around so that the auto came within inches of Ketter. ''Right behind you,'' he repeated.

It took Ketter several minutes to bring his breathing under control after Killebrew had driven away.

He had blown the smoke down the hole and now he could hear the quarry choking and coughing. Soon it would emerge, fangs bared, and Ketter knew he must prepare himself.

Ketter came at a time when he knew no one would disturb them. Bobby lay on the bed in much the same position he had held for weeks. Ketter knew he was washed and manipulated on a regular basis, but the inertness of his posture made him seem as immobile as a statue. It was the first time Ketter had been alone with his friend since he started the hunt.

Holding hands, Ketter gazed into Bobby's eyes. Fixed and flat as mirrors, there was no sign of life behind them. The results of the lie detector test had depressed Ketter enormously. All along, despite all the evidence to the contrary, he had clung to the notion that somehow Bobby was still behind those eyes, his brain functioning normally, trying to get out. Now, at last, Ketter no longer thought so.

''I've done all I can do, Bobby,'' he said. ''The next move is up to the killer. I will try to keep the pressure on, try to get him to panic, but it's up to him. I don't really have anything, and he might know it. It could have been any one of them. They could have done it all together. It could be somebody else entirely. I don't know, I just don't know. All I can do now is keep stomping around, making lots of noise, and hoping he'll panic. The bastard has perfect camouflage, and I'm never going to see him unless he moves. If he never moves, he'll get away with it.''

Ketter looked away from Bobby's face. The feeling of failure was oppressive and bitter. He clutched a fistful of sheet.

"He moved when he attacked you. You were getting close, or he thought you were. I didn't see him move because I wasn't paying attention. Maybe he'll move again if he thinks I'm getting close. It worked for him once. I don't know what else to do. I just don't know what else there is.''

The night outside the window seemed impenetrably dark. Since his encounter with Killebrew, Ketter had gone with great caution by day and night. He was used to caution, but not to the sensation of being hunted; or if not hunted, then certainly watched.

"Did you know about Mike, Bobby? Did you know about my son?'' Ketter stood over his friend and felt as if something inside himself was ripping apart. "Why did it have to be him? Why my boy? Is it my fault? Good God, Bobby, is it my fault?''

Something in his chest burst open and Ketter began to cry. He did not try to stop it although a part of himself was amazed that it was happening. That he did it so openly in front of Bobby was only further proof that he no longer considered his friend truly alive. Ketter cried until he began to sob, great aching moans tearing at him, convulsing his body. He cried for his son, for the pain he felt and must feel in the future. He cried for Bobby, for the secret life he had been forced to lead, for the love he had felt for other men and never been able to express openly, for the life cut short. And he cried most of all for himself, weeping for his inability to comfort his son when the boy needed it most, for the great disappointment he felt in himself. He had failed everyone, it seemed: wife, son, friend, community, self.

When he stopped at last, Ketter felt an enormous sense of release. He dried his eyes on Bobby's sheets, then patted his friend's hand.

"You always were a good listener," he said, smiling. "Do you suppose this means I'm human, after all?" He laughed at himself, feeling all at once lighter, younger, freer.

"Goodbye, Bobby. Goodbye, my good friend," he said, bending to kiss Bobby on the cheek. He knew as he did so that he would not see Bobby again. There was no point in visiting the dead.

Chapter 12

On the day that Bobby Hauck died my father came home early. He visited Ellen Hauck next door for a long while, then came to our house. My mother embraced him wordlessly as he entered the door, and they held each other for several minutes. My mother had been crying since she heard the news, as much in anticipation of my father's grief, I thought, as from her own.

But my father did not appear to be grieving. He was solemn, quiet, sad, but he gave no sign of a man in suffering. If anything, he seemed preoccupied, as if Bobby's death were of only passing interest to him, a momentary distraction from something far more important. As usual, I misjudged my father.

"I need an hour," he said after he finished his embrace with my mother. "Then I want you to come with me, Mike."

"Where?"

"I'm going to change my clothes," he said and started up the stairs.

"It was a blessing, really," my mother said. "At least he's not in pain anymore."

My father turned on the stairs. His voice was suddenly quivering with anger. "He was forty-one years old. It is not a blessing to die at forty-one, it's a tragedy. It's a theft of life. Don't tell me it's a blessing, don't ever say anything like that again. It was murder."

"I only meant because he was . . ."

"I know what you meant. He was murdered. He didn't want to die. He had his skull crushed, deliberately, by another man. Don't ever paint his death as anything but what it was. Murder."

When he came back downstairs, he was dressed in his work clothes. He went out to the stump and began to hack at it with the ax, his body moving in a smooth, unhurried rhythm that looked as if it could go on forever. He worked without pause and after five minutes the back of his shirt was dark with sweat.

People had already started coming to the house, paying their respects to my father as if it were understood that he was the chief mourner. He greeted none of them, but worked unceasingly at the stump. I was not even certain he knew they were there. His whole concentration seemed riveted to the job at hand.

My mother greeted the arrivals and ushered them into the house, where she chatted in hushed tones, acting as if my father's form of grief were perfectly ordinary and understandable under the circumstances.

After an hour, he stopped work abruptly and came back into the house. His work shirt clung to his torso as if it had been sprayed with a hose. Sweat ran in streams from his face and he was crimson from the exertion, but he had about him a look of grateful peace that would have seemed impossible an hour earlier.

I sat in the living room, dutifully conversing with the visitors along with my mother. I had no experience of grief, no familiarity with small talk. They seemed to assume that I, too, was in grief because my father was, where in reality I felt primarily uncomfortable. Death did not seem a reality to me yet, I was too young. There was no sense of finality about it. I lowered my eyes and muttered to them, giving an impersonation of sorrow that seemed to satisfy them well enough.

When my father came in, a hush fell upon us all. My mother came to her feet and crossed toward him solicitously, and the others looked at him with a sort of respectful awe. I felt that they sensed a sort of vicarious excitement being in the presence of great emotion without actually having to suffer for it. My father disappointed them.

"Hello," he said casually, with a trace of a polite smile, as if he had just interrupted my mother's bridge game. He turned to me where I sat uncomfortably squeezed between two adults.

"You ready, Mike?"

I leaped to my feet, eager for anything that would take me out of the atmosphere of gloom. He put his arm across my shoulders and I could feel the heavy warmth of his body.

"We'll be back in a few hours," he said to my mother.

"Peter, our guests have all come to pay their respects."

My father looked at the people in the room. Again the little smile twitched at his lips. He seemed politely amused, as if she had told him they came to burn incense and read tarot cards.

"Thank you," he said. "We all must mourn in our own way. Thank you for coming." He led me out of the house, and I could feel the shock and indignation roil after us like a wave.

We drove the few blocks to Stone Street and parked behind his old office. He sat motionless behind the wheel for a moment, his hands still gripping the steering wheel. He drove, always, with both hands on the wheel. Like a race driver, he explained once. Not that he was worried about himself, but because there were so many idiots on the road. Finally he let his hands drop from the wheel to his lap.

"Mike," he said, his voice distant and soft. "I am not the man I want to be. There's the man I appear to be, and there's the man I really am. That is an enormously hard lesson to learn. And when you learn it, it is hard not to hate yourself for the difference."

I had no idea what he meant, but I did understand that he wasn't really talking to me.

"Bobby did not hate himself for the difference," he added.

We sat in silence for a time. It sounded to me as if he intended his statement to be an epitaph for Bobby and that he was now doing his mourning in the car, with me as the only witness, but I was wrong.

When we got out of the car he walked toward the hardware store that was at the end of the block, next to one of the town's four barbers. "The ladies can dress in black and speak in whispers if they want to," he said, "but I'm not ready to bury Bobby yet."

We entered the hardware store, redolent with its own unique smells of metal and oil. In the back of the store, in a glass case above the counter, were the guns. We stopped there and I looked questioningly at the guns, then at him.

"I can't teach you with any certainty how to live your life," he said. "You're going into territory I know nothing about." He nodded toward the store owner, who hurried toward us with the peculiar respect other men usually paid my father. "But I can teach you what I do know about," he said. Then to the store owner he said, "We want a rifle."

We bought a Remington .22 with a bolt action. It was a boy's rifle, nothing large, nothing fancy. I wanted something bigger and more impressive, but my father knew exactly what he was after.

"This will kill anything you want to kill," he said. "If you need more gun, you're not shooting straight."

He drove us to the Muddy, stopping first to buy two six-packs of canned soda. He showed me how to load it, sliding one Long Rifle cartridge after another into the loading tube, then yanking a shell into the chamber with the action of the bolt.

We drank one of the sodas, then set up the others in a row on the opposite side of the river. After I had learned to hit the stationary targets with a fair degree of accuracy, he tossed them one by one into the water and had me try to hit them before they were carried downstream or sunk.

"You've got the nerves for it," he said after a while. "You hold it steady, squeeze slowly, and you hit what you aim at. It's good shooting. Whether or not you've got the stomach for it is another question. I hope you don't find out."

I could tell from the sudden darkness of his tone that he was not talking about shooting squirrels and rabbits.

"The thing about a .22," he continued, "is that it doesn't make a much bigger hole going in than coming out. A bone will stop it, lots of things will stop it. To kill with it, you must hit the exact spot or keep shooting until the target falls. Like this."

He took the rifle from me and tossed the last of the cans into the water. He shot and the can jerked violently downstream. The second shot followed the first almost immediately and lifted the can completely out of the water. Shot after shot, working the bolt almost as fast as he could pull the trigger, he propelled the can along the surface of the water, never giving it time enough to sink. We had just reloaded and he emptied all fourteen shots into the can without pause or hesitation.

"Like that," he said, putting the rifle back in my hands. The barrel was burning hot to the touch. "Now all you have to do is learn how to do that if the can is shooting back."

I stumbled once on the way back to the car and he reached out to steady me. His hand held my arm, then he let it slide around my shoulders. We walked to the car that way. It felt so good I wanted to lay my head upon his chest and have him comfort me, but of course I did not, not daring to ask for more than the moment gave.

I was reluctant to get into the car, not wanting to break the contact. He seemed to sense it, for he turned me to face him, holding me by the shoulders.

*To my amazement, his face was wrinkled with the effort
to keep from crying. He pulled me into his arms and I
heard a sobbing groan escape him.*

"I love you, Mike," he said, as he hugged me.

My father hugged me.

"I love you."

It was then that I broke my resolve and began to cry.

On the day following Bobby Hauck's death, Frank Maust
returned home from work to find Ketter strolling casually
out of the front door. In his arms he carried a kitchen-
drawer divider filled with knives. Ketter did not speak to
Maust when addressed, nor explain himself in any way,
but got into his car and drove away as if Maust did not
exist.

In his house, Maust found his wife in the kitchen,
cleaning up.

"What the hell was Ketter doing here?" Maust
demanded.

"He said he wanted our knives for his investigation."

"And you *gave* them to him?"

"Was there any reason not to, Frankie?" He found her
smugness unbearable.

That night Maust received a call from the night watch-
man at his plant informing him that an unidentified
prowler had been in Maust's office. Maust arrived with a
policeman to find his office ransacked. Nothing appeared
to have been stolen, but a lower drawer was jammed.
When Maust managed to wrench it free, he found it had
been obstructed by a kitchen paring knife that was taped
to the bottom of the drawer above. Dried blood was on
the blade and the wooden handle. Maust started to show
it to the policeman, but thought better of it.

Driving home in the night following a Rotary club meeting, Walter Stimpf noticed headlights following him in the

distance. He deliberately took a wrong turn and stopped his car to see if the other would follow. He watched his mirror closely, looking for the twin lights to round the corner. They did not come. Relieved, Stimpf drove on. As he approached his driveway, lights came on only a few feet behind him. He realized with fright that the other car had been following him for some time, driving without lights, virtually invisible in the night. The car swerved away from Stimpf and drove off. In the darkness, Stimpf could not identify the car. He called the police, realizing the futility of the gesture as he did it.

On the day of Bobby's funeral, Edward Ketter escorted his wife from the church to their car and noticed that the trunk was ajar. Edward glanced into the trunk before closing it securely. He did not speak to Etta on the ride home, but drove into the garage and waited for the automatic door to close before getting out of the car. Alone in the garage he opened the trunk and lifted up the rug that covered the spare tire and the other tools he carried for emergencies. The shovel was gone. To make sure, he searched the garage where rakes, hoes, and power tools hung neatly on hooks, their outlines chalked on the walls. The shovel was nowhere to be found.

He slept fitfully and awoke when he thought he heard a noise from the garage. Edward took his 12-gauge shotgun from his den, loaded it, and walked to the garage without turning on any lights. He burst through the garage door, at the same time snapping on the light. There was no one there. The overhead light made him squint and the silence of the garage seemed to mock him. As he walked through the garage, he had the sense that someone was watching but he could not tell from where.

He stopped with a gasp when he saw the missing shovel, hanging from its appointed hooks. He looked at it closely with a chill running up his spine. There was a dark spot where the metal met the wooden handle.

Edward took the shovel into the kitchen, keeping the
shotgun close by him on the countertop. The spot
appeared to be dried blood, just a trace, almost enough
not to have noticed. He scrubbed it fastidiously in the
kitchen sink.

Two days later Harry Killebrew felt something sticking
him through the seat of his squad car. He pulled out the
cushion after some difficulty and discovered a kitchen
knife hidden deep within the frame of the seat. It had
bloodstains on it.

Chapter 13

After he taught me to shoot, my father and I went out frequently together to take target practice at the river. We did not actually hunt anything—he said that hunting was a solitary art, and he didn't want any part of it in any event—but we both enjoyed our forays. My instruction period was over. He either thought I knew what he had to teach, or else he felt there was no further point in trying to educate me; but there were no more homilies, no lectures, no instructive anecdotes. We went as two men together, just out to have a good time. He had accepted me as a man and as a person, and I, as far as a teenager ever can, accepted my father as a person.

We grew closer with each foray together, and they were, without question, the happiest days of my youth. And although it was sometimes hard to tell with my father, I think they were happy days for him, too. I was not the son he might have wished for. I was no man's notion of an ideal son, but I had become the only son he had and I did not feel he wanted to trade me in.

By late October the land around Cascade had turned a dull brown. The crops were harvested, the remaining stubble sere and lifeless. Without the sighing waves of corn, there was once again nothing to block the horizon except the slow undulation of the ground itself. The leaves on the trees lining the banks of the Muddy had fallen and only a few remained, trapped under the surface of the little eddies, fading and rotting into silt.

"The Indians that used to live here tell a story about this part of the world," my father told me as we drove one Saturday toward the river. "When the Great Spirit sat upon the face of the earth, He fashioned great mountains and green valleys, places where there were huge canyons, and forests that stretched forever. He scooped out mighty oceans and pinched rivers into waterfalls. In the sandy places He sculpted peaks and buttes and mesas as signs of His presence. Everywhere He turned His hand, He fashioned majesty and beauty. When He was finished, He arose and returned to the Spirit Land, leaving a world of astonishing beauty—except for one place." His arm swept around us, taking in the barren, featureless land. "This," he said with a grin, "is where He sat."

We were laughing when it happened, I remember that very clearly. The sound of my father's laughter was rare and welcome, an event to be cherished. He had his arm around my shoulders and I knew that I was loved.

Like a monster born of earth and leaves, he rose up from a depression in the riverbank, his shotgun pointed at us, his face like death. It took seconds, or fractions of seconds, for it to register on me, but my father saw him as he moved. His first instinct was for my safety, and he pushed me aside with great force. I tripped on a furrow and fell, but even as I went down my mind registered odd, irrelevant details: the monster had been lying there for some time; the leaves under him were pressed flat, which meant he knew where we would come; there were leaves on his head and several stuck to his featureless face—he had tried to camouflage himself completely—even the shotgun was partially masked with more leaves and twigs applied to it to change the outline.

My father must have been expecting it in some way, for he not only reacted instantly, but with great directness, as if he had formed a plan for this emergency long ago.

As I hit the ground I saw him leap in the other direction, one hand going to his back. With the first roar of the shotgun I closed my eyes. When I opened them again, I realized, as much as I could realize anything, that the shot had missed us both. The hand that my father had reached behind his back came forward and magically a pistol had materialized in it. It was his left hand, which is probably why he missed with his first shot.

The monster turned the shotgun directly at my father, who lay without cover on the barren field. He had no face, only eyes and a crimson slash for a mouth. There were no ears, no nose, no hair. The shotgun roared and the ground around my father seemed to come to life, as if the dirt were raining upward. My father stiffened, then slumped.

"Dad!" I screamed.

The monster seemed to notice me for the first time. He swiveled toward me and pulled the trigger but nothing happened. He dug in his pocket for more shells as I wasted precious seconds with stunned inaction. My own rifle had fallen from my grasp when I hit the ground. I grabbed it by the barrel and ran. In my panic, I ran the wrong way, away from the car, deeper into the empty field.

I heard the blast of the gun again and felt a stinging on the back of my head. Dimly I understood that I had been hit but that I had already outrun the effective range of the shotgun. He might hit me from this distance, but the pellets would be too widely spread and too weak to kill me.

I glanced back and saw the man—for I knew he was just a man, a killer in a ski mask and a camouflage jacket—lumbering after me on an angle, chasing me, but at the same time placing himself directly between me and the car.

He lifted the shotgun and aimed it carefully. I threw myself on the ground. With a laugh that was both trium-

phant and filled with contempt for my stupidity, he kept running, gaining yards as I scrambled up again.

I ran in sheer panic, looking back over my shoulder, stumbling across the furrows. There was no place to run except all the way back to town, we were far from the road, from houses, from shelter and safety. He was older and out of shape, and I gained steadily, increasing my lead and making his shotgun less and less effective.

The wire caught me in the stomach and across the legs, the barbs tearing at my clothes and skin as I fell. My arm was caught on one strand of the fence wire and a barb tore across my face from chin to scalp. Stunned and immobilized as if I had been kicked in the stomach, I lay there for a couple of seconds, trying to stop the world from reeling. He came at me with thudding steps and hoarse breath. As he raised the shotgun, I heard a shot and saw him grab at his hip. My father was too far away for a pistol to be either accurate or deadly, but he had hit his mark. The man turned toward my father, then looked down in amazement at the blood coming through his fingers. My father fired again and the man dived to the ground as I crawled under the bottom strand of wire.

There was a fringe of high weeds under the fence where the mower could not reach, and I burrowed into the ground on the other side, praying the weeds would hide me.

I knew that the man was still alive, I had seen that as I crawled away. I also realized that my father could not walk, or he would already have done so, coming close enough to stop the man while still staying out of range of the shotgun.

Like a child hiding his eyes in the belief that he cannot be seen because he cannot see, I tried to press myself deep into the earth. When I looked, I could see only weeds and I prayed that the man could see no more of me. I waited for him to come; then, at long last, my mind began to work with some clarity. He did not come, I realized, because he feared me, and the reason he feared me, the thing I had completely ignored, was that I had a weapon. My rifle, still unfired, lay beside me, the metal barrel cold in my hand. I had carried it instinctively the whole time, clinging to it the way a frightened child might clutch a blanket. The killer thought more of me than I had thought of myself. If he did not come directly to the fence to finish me, it was because he could not see me and did not realize I was too frightened to know I could shoot back.

As I eased the rifle into position in front of me, I understood that the killer had a problem. With my father wounded but still armed, the killer was outgunned. His shotgun did not have the effective range of my father's pistol. What he needed, so he could finish my father without further endangering himself, was a long-range weapon. My rifle.

I knew he would come, but I also knew there was something I could do about it, and with that knowledge came my first bit of courage. My eyes bored through the weeds and I listened as I had never listened before. I did not need to remember the lessons my father had taught me—survival was teaching me anew and with a greater urgency.

At first there were only browns, the earth, the weeds, the faded grasses, the gnarled wood of the fence post. I moved my eyes, roaming back and forth over the section in front of me, trying to catch a hint of patterns, attempting to discern the camouflaged bulk of the killer.

I heard him first, changing position, dragging his knees under him. When he came, he would have to come quickly, not only to surprise me but also to evade my father's fire. My eyes reacted to my ears and saw the slightest movement. He was no more than fifteen yards away. He had but to pull the trigger and splatter me into the ground; that he hadn't could only mean he didn't know exactly where I was. His uncertainty was my only advantage. If I moved to prepare for him, he could detect me just as I had seen him. I forced myself to lie perfectly *still, to wait until he committed himself before swinging the rifle around. I could not even remember if there was a shell in the chamber of my rifle. Rather than risk it, I would have to work the bolt action once before firing. I felt like a rabbit hunkering in the shadow of a hawk, counting on immobility as my only defense.*

Suddenly he came, without any further warning. I rolled and yanked at the bolt and he was at the fence line, firing down at where he thought I was. The ground exploded two inches from my leg and earth showered up. I pointed the gun at his chest as he moved his shotgun upward toward my body. He jerked sideways suddenly in reaction to what I later realized was my father's bullet catching him in the shoulder. Still deafened by the first shotgun blast, I had not heard my father's shot. Nor did I hear my own, but I kept firing and pumping the bolt and firing again until the man fell and did not move.

I wanted to carry my father straight to the car, but he insisted on first learning who the killer had been. I helped him to the man's fallen body and yanked off the ski mask. Frank Maust's fat face stared vacantly at the sky.

My father nodded once, as if in confirmation, before I carried him to the car and the hospital.

And so my father made the headlines one more time before we left Cascade for good. I am off in the world as I so longed to be, and he and my mother have moved on to another small town in another state where he can be just another attorney, a nice man with a severe limp, nothing about him to suggest the hunter or the prey.